The first step
to heartbreak . . .

Laura tiptoed to her husband's side. Unfortunately, she passed too close to the table and something crashed to the floor.

"Who is there?" Eric questioned, his hand reaching automatically toward the bandages that swathed his eyes.

"It is only I, my love," Laura said softly.

"Oh, Julia, my dear," Eric said happily, "I was wondering if you would come."

Laura stepped back from the bed, her heart pounding in her throat. It was on the tip of her tongue to enlighten her husband on the one characteristic Laura shared with her beautiful sister—that soft, slightly husky voice, so beguiling when it issued from Julia's lovely lips. Instead she said, "But Eric, dear, you knew I must . . ."

The Benevolent Bride

PAMELA FRAZIER

B

BERKLEY BOOKS, NEW YORK

THE BENEVOLENT BRIDE

A Berkley Book/published by arrangement with
the author

PRINTING HISTORY
Berkley edition/April 1989

ISBN: 0-425-11534-8

A BERKLEY BOOK © TM 757.375
Berkley Books are published by the Berkley Publishing Group,
200 Madison Avenue, New York, NY 10016
The name "BERKLEY" and the "B" logo
are trademarks belonging to the Berkley Publishing Corporation

PRINTED IN THE UNITED STATES OF AMERICA

10 9 8 7 6 5 4 3 2 1

ONE

"WHERE IS SHE?" Lady Roswell said in ascending tones as she stalked down the upstairs hall. She had just glanced into the library, and now she closed the door of the music room with just the suggestion of a slam. Lady Roswell was known for her forbearance in times of stress. Her daughters, the ladies Margaret and Julia, had reason to appreciate this quality in their mother. She had a reputation of being just and fair-minded, and her charm had opened many a door, usually closed to widows, no matter what their status. She was as popular with Queen Charlotte as she was with the Prince Regent, and even the unhappy Princess Caroline had, before she fled London for the Continent, found Lady Roswell one of the few peeresses with whom she felt at ease. Consequently it was a source of constant annoyance to her ladyship that despite her reputation for soothing the most turbulent of waters and setting the most difficult matters to right, she had little or, rather, no success in rendering her youngest daughter, Lady Laura, fully cognizant of her position in life and, more specifically, this household.

"Where is she?" Lady Roswell repeated, a kindling eye on the stairs to the third floor and continuing up to the attic. Her question was, of course, rhetorical, for she knew full well that her recalcitrant daughter was in the attic, unmindful of the dust and probably near one of the windows, which meant that she would have displaced boxes, pushed piles of dusty curtains aside, and in the process dirtied her gown and herself.

"Neither of your sisters," Lady Roswell said icily to Laura, who was indeed by the window in the attic, "ever would have dreamed of coming up here! What, pray, is the matter with the library or the parlor?" Without giving her youngest child a chance to reply, she continued, "Your grandmother will be here this afternoon at four, which gives you no more than an hour to prepare yourself. I vow, you are dust from head to foot! Your gown is filthy! There are smudges on your cheek—one would think you were a ragamuffin playing in the dirt rather than my daughter!" She allowed the suggestion of a sob to color her tones. "I am glad your poor father could not see you. I cannot begin to imagine what he would have thought!"

"I am sure"—Laura put down her book and looked up at her mother—"that he would not have thought anything, Mama. He would not have known me, since he died a month before I was born."

"Oh!" Lady Roswell exclaimed, clasping her hands to her bosom in a gesture redolent of Mrs. Siddons as the Tragic Muse. "How can you be so insensitive as to remind me?"

Laura said, "What do you want with me now, Mother?"

"Did I not tell you this morning after you returned from riding that your grandmother would be here at five this afternoon and that she wishes to see you?"

"It is not four yet," Laura pointed out reasonably. "It lacks two hours of being five. When I came up here, I fully intended to come downstairs at four so that Lucy could dress me."

"Can you imagine that it will take Lucy but an hour to dress *you?*" Lady Roswell demanded sarcastically. "Look at your hair and the dirt all over you. You will have to bathe, and your hair must be washed and you know how long it takes to dry, being so thick and worn far too long. You must come down from there this minute. I will not have your grandmother tell me again that it is shocking the way you go about. You could be some blacksmith's daughter or—"

"Please, Mama." Laura rose reluctantly. "I will come, though why I must be presented at court and brought out, I cannot know. I am out already—at least I have been seen in and around London and I have acquaintances here, and despite what Grandmother says, I am reasonably sure that in or out, no man is going to offer for me. You have said that yourself often enough, and so have Margaret and Julia. They have not hesitated to quote the opinions of their friends, and also those of their husbands. I know very well that I am not a matrimonial prospect, and I do wish I could return to the country, where I was comfortable. I am entirely reconciled to being a maiden lady, and there is certainly more room to ride at home."

"Neither your grandmother nor myself," Lady Roswell said firmly, if not quite truthfully, "are prepared to write you off at eighteen. You come from excellent stock and your portion is large. I, or rather we, are of the opinion that some young man will be delighted to offer for you."

"I have seen no evidence of that delight." Laura rose, futilely brushing some cobwebs from her skirt and clutching to her bosom the book she had been reading. "We know quite a few young men at the Hall, and while they have clustered around my sisters like so many bees around honeysuckle, at least before they were married, I have yet to notice any clustering around me. The only compliments I have received were regarding my seat on a horse and . . . oh, yes, young Mr. Beauchamps said he was pleased because I did not scream when I fell into the water jump. I do not imagine that suggests any lurking desire to become my husband."

"You are pleased to be ironic," Lady Roswell commented. She wished that she did not have to look up at her daughter. It was much easier to give a set-down to one smaller than oneself, and Laura could give her at least three inches in height. She continued doggedly. "You do remind me of your father in that, to be sure. I will tell you that it is no one's fault but your own that you are not as graceful as your sister Julia, or as charming. You do not make the effort. You sit quietly in a corner, and how often have I come to find you surreptitiously reading—when you imagine that you are unobserved."

"I never imagine that I am unobserved, Mama. I *know* I am unobserved. I could read the whole of Mr. Boswell's *Biography of Samuel Johnson* and no one would be the wiser. No one looks my way when Julia is in the room.

"Julia is married."

"I have been in her drawing room when there are unmarried young men about, and they still look at her unceasingly. The only things that Julia and I have in common are our voices."

"That is true. I mean," Lady Roswell said crossly, "that they are amazingly similar, but that is not unusual. My voice was similar to that of my sister." Lady Roswell frowned and continued. "I have told her over and over again that she ought not to court the attentions of young, unmarried men—but that is aside from the point. Come down and have Lucy see what she can do with you."

"Very well, Mama." Laura followed her mother out of the attic. "But I think we are in agreement that it will not be much."

Precisely at the hour of four, Laura stood in the center of the drawing room feeling acutely uncomfortable as, at the direction of her grandmother, the dignified Countess of Ormonde, she pivoted for the second time. "Very well, you may stand still," said the countess, fixing a glacial gray eye on her. In a tone that matched and even exceeded her gaze in coldness, she said, "I can see no resemblance to my son, either."

Lady Roswell said with a matching chill, "She has Edward's eyes. If you will look at them, you will see that they are precisely the same shade of violet."

The countess raised a quizzing glass, which magnified one eye in a most startling manner. "Well, perhaps," she finally allowed. "As I have always said, there is precious little else to remind me of poor, poor Edward. I thought she might grow to resemble her sisters more, as she became older. Unfortunately that has not happened. How did she get to be so heavy? I do not recall that she was so heavy the last time I was here."

"I do not know." Lady Roswell sighed. "She does not have a great appetite. Again, I would say that she takes after your side of the family." There was a certain melancholy satisfaction in her tone that brought her an icy glare from the countess.

Glancing down at her own svelte shape, the latter said, "It is possible that she takes after her uncle. Arthur was on the heavy side. He ate a great deal, as I remember. He also had two chins. She glared at Laura. "Hold your head up, girl."

Laura had a strong impulse to refuse. Words had been piling up in her throat for the past quarter of an hour. She would have given much to tell her tiny but commanding grandmother that she was being unkind, and rude as well. She also would have liked to point out the futility of the presentation they had in mind, but the repercussions were too dreadful to contemplate. One never, never, contradicted her grandmother; one never even made a comment. One was required to listen and eventually to murmur a soft yes or no in answer to questions that rode roughshod over one's feelings. Generally the countess did not question. She stated.

She said now, "I have already made arrangements for the presentation. I have also made appointments with the mantua maker. I have decided upon Mrs. Bell. The woman gets entirely too much notice in her husband's monthly journal, but she is not without taste, and she is particularly adept at clothing young women with difficult figures and no claim to beauty. I have explained Laura's problems to her, and she has already begun to make the

preliminary sketches. I have also told her to prepare one
of her famous Circassian corsets for Laura. Why are you
making such a face, child?"

"I . . . I do not find corsets comfortable," Laura dared
to protest.

"I am sure they are not, but you have no choice, not
with your protruding belly. The gown will have to be
white for the presentation. However, the ball gown
might have a Grecian border at the hem and perhaps
some decoration down the middle to minimize her
unfortunate contours. Her hair will have to be cut and
shaped. I will have my hairdresser attend to that."

"Or mine," Lady Roswell suggested.

She received a lightning glance from her mother-in-
law. "Well, possibly," she allowed. "I do not believe we
will let her wear jewelry."

"No, certainly not," agreed Lady Roswell. "I would
not even allow Julia to wear jewelry for her first ball."

"It is a pity your girls are not more of a sameness," the
countess said tartly, quite as if she were blaming her
daughter-in-law for the difference.

"I had not the ordering of that," Lady Roswell said
defensively.

"No, 'tis a pity," the countess returned coldly. "I will
procure her a voucher for Almack's, once the presentation is over." She looked at Laura and shook her head.
"Were it not for Jane . . ."

"What about Jane?" Lady Roswell demanded sharply.
"You will not be telling me that all this . . . this pother is
based on one of Jane's predictions?"

The countess said, "But of course, it is, my dear. As
she did with your other two daughters, she has predicted
that Laura will marry within three months of her presentation at Court. I have asked that that take place at the
beginning of May, which means that she ought to be off
your hands by August at the latest. The wedding will be
held at St. James's Church, and I, of course, will have the
reception at my house."

"Ouf!" Laura could not help the exclamation that

escaped her. She did manage to bite down a hysterical giggle, but the first sound had been enough to bring her grandmother's icy gaze back to her face. "What did you wish to say, Laura?"

Laura swallowed convulsively. "My . . . my two sisters are . . . are neither one like me. It . . . it is possible that Jane did not take that into account."

"Jane," the countess said coldly, "is the great-granddaughter of a woman who was executed for witchcraft. Her powers have been passed down to several members of her family, and Jane's predictions have always been uncannily accurate. I was at my wit's end when I asked her about you because, quite frankly, I could not imagine that you would ever have the slightest chance of being wed. Contrary to my expectations, Jane said . . . but I have already told you what she said. Your first appointment will be at three tomorrow. Your mother will accompany you, of course. I adjure you both, do not be late."

Laura waited until her grandmother had gone. Then, turning to her mother, she said succinctly, "Damn Jane."

For once Lady Roswell did not protest either Laura's language or frankness. "I have more than a feeling that that must have taken place already. The woman is, as your grandmother has stated, most uncannily accurate, and not only at predicting marriages. She warned me regarding your poor father's early demise, and on other matters as well. Indeed, I would not be surprised to learn that she and the devil are on intimate terms."

It occurred to Laura that the countess, too, might enjoy that infernal intimacy. However, despite all the portents, she was positive that the devil was wrong this time.

On the third Wednesday of May 1816, the venerable halls of Almack's were filled with those members of the ton fortunate enough to pass the scrutiny of its hostesses and thus procure a voucher for the weekly subscription ball. A great many gentlemen were on the floor going through the paces of a country dance. Others stood at the sidelines of the ballroom scrutinizing those young ladies who were dancing. Often their scrutiny was aided by quizzing glasses. None of those gentlemen—at least none of the handsome young men who thronged the halls—had so much as a glance at the several rows of chairs, where other young ladies, accompanied by their chaperones, sat stiffly at attention. Though they were doing their best to look pleasant, hope, never very strong in the first place, dwindled quickly.

Laura, who had been one of this unhappy group for a half hour this night, and for several hours the preceding Wednesday, did not join them in casting wistful glances at the floor. Despite the prodding of Lady Howard, a distant connection of her late father, she sat reading Maria Edgeworth's *Essay on Irish Bulls,* which she was enjoying even more than *Castle Rackrent.* They were both older books—at least sixteen or seventeen years had passed since their publication—but they had escaped her attention until recently, and as she read, she was having trouble in keeping herself from laughing aloud.

"Laura," Lady Howard snapped. "No one will ask you to dance if you sit there looking down at your book!"

Laura managed to swallow an annoyed rejoinder. She said, "No one, Lady Howard, will ask me whether I look up or down—and I much prefer to read. I am *enjoying* my book."

"You are not here to read," Lady Howard persisted.

"Judging from my experience last Wednesday, when I did not read, I am not here to dance, either. It does become exceptionally boring just to sit here for two hours having nothing to do."

"Some gentleman might . . ." Lady Howard began hopefully.

"I beg your pardon, Lady Howard," Laura said bluntly, "but some gentleman will not. There are girls here on the chairs who have much the advantage of me in looks, and no one asks them, either."

"They do not have the advantage of you," Lady

Howard responded in a low voice. "If you were thinner, you would be exceptionally well-looking."

"I am not thinner," Laura replied with an uncompromising finality. She stubbornly turned her gaze on her book.

Eric Delamore, Lord Marne, standing at the side of the dance floor, fixed a lackluster stare on the numerous young women, now in the midst of a cotillion. With a slight shudder he turned away, thinking wistfully of the card room. He had more than half a mind to go there at once, despite the fact that he had faithfully promised his sister, Celia, and his godmother, Lady Cavendish, that he would ask some female to dance.

"Will you remain secluded for the rest of your life?" Lady Cavendish had questioned, speaking with the freedom of one who had known him since babyhood.

Actually it was not a question, but an order disguised as a question. In effect she had been saying, "As the last of the Marnes, Eric, it is your duty to marry again." She had gone on to say in actuality, "I know you loved poor dear Christina to distraction, and I know you were eagerly anticipating the birth of your first child. It is extremely unfortunate that she died in childbed, and the poor baby with her. Yes, I know it was a boy, a double misfortune. I do not say that you should forget her or your love—but it has been close on three years, and it is time you thought of the title. It would be a shame to let it lapse."

"Damn the title!" he muttered to that imposing presence situated in his mind's eye. He sent a brief prayer to the Almighty, thanking Him for giving her the touch of quinsy that had prevented her from accompanying him this night and choosing eligible partners for him. He sent up another prayer because his sister had also been prevented from attending the ball. Her husband truly hated Almack's and the hostesses, whom he characterized collectively as being "too damned full of themselves."

Lord Marne agreed with him wholeheartedly, even

though the ladies had been exceedingly cordial to him. Princess Lieven's greeting had hinted at something more, did he wish to avail himself of the opportunity. That it was a heavily weighted opportunity which was certainly predicated on his connection with the House of Lords and the hope that her artful questions might extract some bit of useful information that she might pass on to her husband, the Russian ambassador, did lessen the excitement she promised. However, he had smilingly appeared not to comprehend her charming smile and beguiling words, and he could only hope that he had not made an enemy for life. The time was past when he wanted to complicate his life with a dangerous intrigue.

Just as that thought left his mind, he replaced it with another that certainly should have occurred to him earlier. Since neither his godmother nor his sister were here this night, why had he come in the first place? He did not want to look for a bride; he did not want to be married again, not yet. He would leave now. He started for the door, but unfortunately he caught sight of Lady Craven, a dear friend of his sister's. Had she seen him? If she had not, there was every possibility that she would see him as he passed her on his way out, and no doubt his early withdrawal would be communicated to Celia, whom he had promised faithfully that he would attend the ball and remain there for at least an hour.

Muttering an oath under his breath, he sent a harried glance around the room and caught sight of the unfortunate females who occupied the chairs. As he regarded them he was aware of a battery of eyes impaling him, anxious eyes, unhappy eyes, the eyes of those young ladies who had come to Almack's in the vain hope of being asked to dance. He would dance with one of them, and consequently Lady Craven, damn her, could tell his sister that Eric had done his duty.

It was a duty that grew ever more irksome the closer he drew to those hapless, hopeless females. And then, as he, feeling uncomfortably like some Oriental potentate trying to decide which houri he would select for the night,

edged nearer to the chairs, he saw one who was outstand-
ingly different from the others! It was not that she was
prettier. He had no notion of how she looked. Her head
was bent, her eyes fixed on a book! Surely, he decided, it
must be an affectation. No young lady in receipt of a
prized voucher to Almack's would be sitting there reading, rather than casting out lures, such lures as she might
possess! However, this damsel, her eyes fastened on the
printed page, seemed totally unaware of her surround-
ings, totally oblivious to the fact that she was there for a
purpose, a purpose that had nothing to do with reading a
book!

Obviously she could not be well-chaperoned; else she
would have been sternly reprimanded and the book put
away. He glanced at her companion and recognized Lady
Howard, with whom he had a slight acquaintance. Her
head was bent so that he could not catch her eye, but
obviously she must be baffled. Undoubtedly, her charge
had a will of her own. It occurred to him that he would
like to discover the identity of this surprisingly willful
young woman.

Laura, happily perusing a delightful if rather sad little
tale of a cruel Welsh schoolmaster, a hapless Irish lad,
and his kind schoolmate, was being by turns sympathetic
and indignant. Miss Edgeworth wrote with great sympathy for the Irish, and that pleased her. She was put in
mind of Tim O'Toole from County Cork, her riding
master, whom she had greatly missed after his return to
Ireland.

She was in the midst of shaking her head over some
piece of injustice meted out to the Irish boy by the
schoolmaster when a cough caused her to look up swiftly,
expecting . . . she was not sure what. She had entertained a vision of one of her mother's friends finding her
so engaged, but even as she looked up, she realized that it
had not been a feminine but a masculine cough, and then
she stopped thinking about coughs entirely as she met
dark brown eyes set in a face that called up the description "classically handsome." In fact, his features might

even be termed poetically handsome. The dark eyes were large, the nose was beautifully shaped, the mouth was firm, the lips neither too full nor too thin but achieving a perfect median between the two. There was a sharp cleft in his chin, and she noted that his complexion was olive and his cheekbones high. His hair was blue-black, and she had the impression of a felicitous blend of Spanish or Italian mixed with English. Having reached this conclusion, she belatedly realized that she was staring at him, and certainly he was staring at her. She blushed and darted a side glance at Lady Howard, finding her nodding.

"But what are you reading?" the gentleman asked in a low, pleasant voice, his gaze briefly on the somnolent chaperone.

"It's called *An Essay on Irish Bulls.* Maria Edgeworth's the author."

"Ah, she also wrote *Castle Rackrent,* am I right?" he asked.

"Yes, you are." Laura nodded. "That is her most famous book, I believe, but she has written quite a few others. This one has a partially Irish background. I think she once lived in Ireland."

"I have the impression that she still travels back and forth between England and Ireland," he commented.

"Do you know her?" Laura asked interestedly.

"My wife used to be quite fond of her works," he explained.

"Oh, really?" Laura was conscious of a strange little prick of disappointment. Yet of course he would be married, a man of that age. He appeared to be in his mid to late twenties, and he was so singularly attractive! And why should she, of all people, be disappointed? She could not hope to interest him. Probably he was on his way to meet his wife.

He said, "Do you intend to read for the entire evening?"

She decided on the truth, for there was no reason to dissemble. After all, she was speaking to a married man, not that she would have dissembled before—well, she might have in hopes of being asked to dance. That was, of course, a very forlorn hope, a foolish hope, given the appearance of the man standing beside her. She said, "I do not believe I will have an opportunity to do much else save read."

"You might dance." He smiled. "In fact, I believe that the next dance will be a country dance. Might I hope that you will be my partner?"

"Me?" Laura said ungrammatically.

Lady Howard, who had woken in time to hear the last part of this exchange, mentally cringed but said brightly, "Of course she will. She will be delighted."

Laura visited a swift, annoyed look at her chaperone, and then the lady's eagerness brought a smile to her face, a natural smile full of amusement. "I would be delighted to be your partner for the country dance, sir. Except . . ."

"Except what?" he questioned.

"Well, I am a much better horsewoman than I am a dancer. I find the patterns of the dance rather confusing."

"My dear child," Lady Howard protested. "She is all unspoiled, my lord."

"So I see," he said. He added, "Perhaps you will do me the kindness of introducing us, Lady Howard."

"You have not been introduced?" she asked confusedly, and reddened. "Oh, dear, I . . . I fear I am to blame. My . . . er, Laura, my dear, may I present the Earl of Marne. Your lordship, this is Lady Laura Roswell."

"Lady Laura Roswell"—he bowed—"I am delighted to make your acquaintance."

"And I yours, my lord," she murmured.

"May I inscribe my name on one of the spokes of your fan?" he asked, pointing to the little ivory fan that lay folded in her lap.

"You may, of course"—she held it up—"but it is really not necessary. There are no others, and I will remember the next country dance. I will be sitting right here."

"My dear . . ." Lady Howard protested softly.

"I think I will inscribe it, anyway," he said. Taking her fan, he produced a small pencil, with which he wrote his name in a flowing script that Laura thought was the most beautiful handwriting she had ever seen.

"I thank you, my lord," she murmured as he returned the fan.

"It is I who must thank you, Lady Laura." Taking her hand, he pressed a kiss on it. "I will be back directly they announce the country dance." He smiled and bowed.

"Oh, my dearest Laura," Lady Howard breathed as he strode away. "Have you any notion of your good fortune?"

"Yes," Laura said as she stared at her fan, thinking that she would keep it until her dying day.

Meanwhile a veritable babble of conversation had broken out among the girls sitting to her left, her right, behind and before her.

"Oh, you are fortunate," sighed a plain young woman sitting next to Lady Howard. "Imagine dancing with Lord Marne."

Meeting yearning blue eyes set in a plain little face topped by mousy brown curls, Laura said, "Do you know him, then?"

"My brother knew him at Eton," the girl said. "He came home with him once. He was handsome even then."

"He is a very attractive young man," Lady Howard said. She added, "He comes from an old and extremely distinguished family, my dear Laura. And on his mother's side he is distantly related to the de Medici family, which I believe accounts for his darkness."

"I knew his wife," a girl in front of them turned around to say. "At least, my sister did. They were in school together."

"An extremely foolish young woman," Lady Howard frowned.

"Yes, she was," the girl said before Laura could question her chaperone. "My sister said that even in school she would be walking around in a rainstorm reciting poetry."

"But she was beautiful," the girl, with the brother, murmured.

Caught by the past tense, Laura said, "Is his wife no longer living?"

"Alas, no, poor Christina." Lady Howard sighed. "She died in childbed, and the baby with her. He was reported to be inconsolable."

"Oh, dear, what a shame," Laura murmured, feeling a strange exultation that she dared not examine more closely. A second later she did examine it and told herself that she was a goose, a dunce, and mad, besides, to lay even the first brick of a dream castle. The handsome young Earl of Marne was not for the likes of an overweight damsel with her nose in a book while sitting in the chairs at Almack's. He was only being kind, and after tonight undoubtedly she would never see him again. Indeed, she could count herself fortunate if, after all, he came back to claim her for the dance—fan or no fan. Resolutely she opened her book at the place she had marked.

TWO

"WHAT IS THIS I AM TOLD?" Lady Roswell said loudly as she pulled up the shades in Laura's bedchamber. Sunlight came blindingly through the windows, battening upon Laura's closed eyelids and reddening the darkness beneath them. Laura, opening her eyes, blinked against that brightness and would have rolled over to bury her face in the pillows had not her mother seized her arm.

"You danced a country dance with Lord Marne?" Lady Roswell questioned.

"Yes . . ." Laura moaned, unhappily reminded of that dance. "I stepped on his foot. I wish he would not have asked me. I much preferred speaking to him. He did not wince, but I cannot think it was very comfortable. I expect that is why I did not see him anymore." She groaned and buried her face in the pillow.

"Sybil tells me that you had quite a conversation with him," Lady Roswell said, appropriating the pillow. "Do wake up, Laura," she continued impatiently. "It is fifteen minutes past the hour of ten, and you have slept quite long enough."

Laura regarded her mother blearily. Generally Lady Roswell did not care how long she slept. She read eagerness and hope in her mother's gaze and had no trouble tracing them to their source. "We conversed about Maria Edgeworth, Mama. I was reading one of her books, and he told me that his wife used to read them too."

"His wife is dead," Lady Roswell said with a satisfaction that Laura, now reluctantly awake, found most inappropriate.

"Yes, that is what Lady Howard told me. She said that he was inconsolable."

"She died two years ago. He has had time to recover from her passing. He is the last of his line, you know."

"I do feel sorry for him," Laura said. "Poor man."

"He is not poor, my dear. He is exceedingly rich and he belongs to a fine family. It is small wonder that his godmother, Lady Cavendish, is anxious for him to marry—his sister Celia too."

"They . . . they want him to marry his *sister?*" Laura sat up straight, staring at her mother incredulously.

"May heaven preserve me!" Lady Roswell exclaimed. "You are not usually so dense, Laura. I said that his sister, Celia, Lady Belmore, wishes him to marry again. She has given birth to twin daughters and cannot have any more children. Consequently, if he does not marry, the line will end with him. He must have an heir!"

"I do not believe that he should be pressed to marry again, at least not immediately," Laura said staunchly. "I have the feeling that he is very unhappy. His smile never reaches his eyes." She added, "I heard last night that his wife was very beautiful."

"She was beautiful and, unfortunately, of a poetical bent, my friend Lady Latimer told me. She had a slight acquaintance with Christina and said that she reminded her of Lady Caroline Lamb, tiny, wispy, and frail. I understand that she was much more beautiful than poor Caroline; but no matter, she loved roaming through the high grass when it was touched with morning dew or some such folderol, and did so even when she was with child with the result that she caught a fever and subsequently died in childbed, losing the child too. Not even Caro Lamb was that silly! But of course, Lady Latimer said, he—Lord Marne—was inconsolable. She had captured his imagination along with his heart. Oh, dear, I do not know why I am giving you all this nonsense. It is far more important that I tell you that you have received a large bouquet of roses from Lord Marne, and he has written that he hopes he may wait upon you this afternoon at three."

"Surely you jest!" Laura cried.

"Of course I do not jest," Lady Roswell responded irritably. "I do not blame you for being surprised. I, too, was surprised—and coming immediately after your second night at Almack's. I think you must wear your blue lutestring, my dear. It does bring out your eyes. Your eyes are, by far, your best feature, Laura, and I suspect they would be larger were you less plump, but they are a lovely color—truly violet. Your hair is pretty too."

"I cannot imagine why he would want to see me again," Laura said wonderingly.

Since Lady Roswell was caught between a hope she hardly dared express even to herself, and a normal confusion, she said vaguely, "I expect he enjoyed talking to you, my dear. You are intelligent and you are not flighty. Furthermore, you are an eligible young lady and—"

"You cannot imagine that he regards me in that light!" Laura exclaimed incredulously.

"Well, no, I really do not imagine that he does," Lady Roswell allowed as she mentally and reluctantly summed up the unlikely aspects of her fugitive hope. "I understand that he is just beginning to go about in society again . . ." She let that comment trail off, adding finally, "I will know better after I have seen him."

Lord Marne, arriving at Lady Roswell's town house at the stated hour of three, approved its classic lines. It had belonged, he knew, to the family for at least two generations and, in common with the daughter of the house, it suggested stability if not beauty. He reminded himself that stability was what he wanted. Laura, large, at least a head taller than dearest Christina (he winced as he considered the contrast), breathed stability. He doubted if there were a flutter in her whole makeup. A memory of Christina's breathless speech, her adorable little half sentences, leaving one to guess just what she might mean, arose in his mind and almost kept him from lifting the knocker. Yet lift it he did, feeling its metal chill against his palm. He was half inclined to put it gently, gently against its plate and leave, but he did not. He let it fall, and the resulting clang was, he thought, a signal.

It was opened immediately by a footman in dark blue livery who gave him an interrogative glance. Once more he hesitated, thinking that he could say he had mistaken the house, but again he did not. He gave his name and was ceremoniously ushered into a well-furnished hall. As he waited for the butler to announce him, he looked about him approvingly. There would be no problem about the dowry, he was sure. He knew the Roswell family to be wealthy. One of the problems of his first marriage had been his Christina's meager portion, something that had mattered not at all to him—but his father, alive at the time, had not been at all pleased. Only Christina's heritage had served to soothe the elder Marne. She had been descended on one side from French aristocrats, who traced their lineage back to the Yves Saint-Cloud who had fought the infidel in Jerusalem, and on the other side to the Greys, that same family that counted among its members the unfortunate Lady Jane Grey.

"If your lordship will come this way, her ladyship is awaiting you in the drawing room."

Lord Marne banished Christina and her connections to that vast area of his mind that she still inhabited and from which she was incessantly summoned. He said, "I thank you," and stood a little taller as he prepared himself for what he decided must be the first step in an unhappily undertaken, but most necessary, courtship.

On his way to the drawing room he had reason to approve a long hall, the walls of which were hung with some excellent paintings. Then they were at what he privately termed the "fatal threshold." His name was announced, and taking a deep breath, he expelled it as he stepped into a tastefully decorated apartment. A swift glance showed him Laura in some blue garment, and Lady Roswell, whom she did not resemble. Undoubtedly Laura took after her father's side of the family. Her mother was small and fair. Laura was, as he had noted last night, darker. Her eyes were deep blue, and her hair was chestnut shot with red lights. She had a lovely complexion, but she was plump, which, he decided, was all to the good. Laura would never remind him of Christina. Indeed, she could have made two of his late wife!

He returned Lady Roswell's warm greeting, bowed over her hand, and subsequently greeted and bowed over the trembling hand of her daughter. Laura, he noted, looked exceedingly ill-at-ease. He was sorry for that. He guessed that her mother's presence was intimidating. No doubt Lady Roswell was already building castles in the air—or perhaps churches. He had a mental sigh for the preliminaries of a courtship, based on necessity rather than passion. If he wished, he could turn this visit into a mere courtesy call and never appear again, or he could let it be the first of a series of visits—formal, interspersed with riding in the park and ultimately an unchaperoned drive in his curricle. He wished that poor Laura, so delightful when she was being herself, was not currently so constrained. Then he was reminded of the book he had brought with him. Breaking the silence that had fallen now that the preliminaries of the visit were at an end, he produced the book, bought that morning in Hatchard's. Holding it up, he said, "I do hope you have not read *Ennui*. It is another work of—"

"Maria Edgeworth!" Laura finished hastily, and then, cowed by a look from her mother, she added awkwardly, "I mean . . ."

"You are right," he said hastily. "It is the work of Maria Edgeworth. Have you read it?"

"Oh, no, I have not," Laura said excitedly. "I do thank you."

Lord Marne, seeing traces of the Laura he had encountered the previous night, smiled as he gave it to her. "You are quite welcome. I hope it does not live up to its title."

"*Ennui?* Oh, I do not believe Miss Edgeworth could ever be boring." Seeing an interrogative look on her mother's face, Laura blushed. "I . . . was reading one of Miss Edgeworth's other books last night—"

"Last night at the ball?" Lady Roswell raised an eyebrow.

"I did not expect that I would be asked to dance," Laura responded bluntly, and then blushed deeply. "I . . . I mean . . ."

"I think," Lord Marne said gently, "that you have altogether too small an opinion of yourself, Lady Laura."

"She is all unspoiled, my lord," Lady Roswell murmured, unconsciously echoing Lady Howard.

"I can see she is," he replied. "I think it charming."

"You do?" Laura blurted, and then blushed deeply again.

"I do," he averred, feeling very sorry for her. Even without knowing Lady Roswell, he could envision the scene that must needs take place after his departure. He had best stay a little longer and talk of matters inconsequential, he decided, even though with every moment he remained in the Roswell house he would be more deeply committed to a plan which, at first, had been rather vague and amorphous. Yet, oddly enough, he felt strangely protective of Laura, almost as protective as he had been of his lovely sylph of a wife. Laura certainly was not lovely, but she was needful and embarrassed and, unless he were being too impossibly conceited, in the throes of her first love.

He stayed and they talked; rather, he and Lady Roswell talked of people they knew. They discussed the Byron scandal which, though several months old, was still a topic to generate comment. Finally he took his leave, but not before he had asked if Laura would care to go riding with him in the park.

"Oh, I most certainly would," Laura cried. "I should like it above all things."

"My dear," Lady Roswell murmured, her manner suggesting that such a burst of enthusiasm ill became her daughter.

Lord Marne, seeing the enthusiasm fade from Laura's face, said hastily, "I am pleased that you have agreed, Lady Laura. I will look forward to our ride."

He took his leave shortly after having made arrangements where and when they would meet. Much to his surprise, he found himself annoyed by Lady Roswell's habit of constantly quelling what he guessed to be Laura's native exuberance. She had been a different person at the ball—different, he reminded himself, until Lady Howard woke. The girl gave promise of being quite delightful when she was not being badgered by her elders. If she were in his household, he would see to it that she would be allowed to be her own person. As the implications inherent in that thought suddenly hit him, he realized that he was very near to a decision that he had originally believed must needs take months or even a year or even two.

"Do not be too hasty," he murmured to himself, belatedly remembering the reasons for a marriage that was based on considerations other than love. He could almost hear his sister telling him that he should wed someone older, someone who understood these arrangements.

"Lady Laura Roswell . . . I know a Julia Roswell, or rather, Julia, Lady Ludlow," Celia commented the day following her brother's visit to Lady Roswell's house. "She had a sizable dowry, I remember, but such a flighty girl. If her sister is anything like Julia . . ."

"I have not had the pleasure of Lady Ludlow's acquaintance," Lord Marne said. "Lady Laura is not flighty. On the contrary, she is quite shy and self-effacing."

"And she is Julia's sister?" Celia looked surprised. Then, before he could respond, she added, "But, wait, there is a third one, not long out of the schoolroom, I should imagine."

"I would think that Lady Laura is no more than eighteen," Lord Marne replied a trace uncomfortably, the whole he waited for a burst of derision from Celia.

"Eighteen to twenty-six," Celia murmured. "Well, you are certainly not old enough to be her father. I always believe it more pleasant when there are some years between a man and a woman. Eight is adequate. It is close on the amount that stretched between you and poor Christina, is it not?"

"She was four years my junior," he said.

"Gracious, I should not have thought so," Celia commented, and flushed. "I mean, she did look exceptionally young, not to say"—her flush deepened—"very young."

Lord Marne, having a good idea of what his sister had meant to say, responded coolly. "I am quite aware of your opinion of Christina. You should have made an effort to know her better."

It was an old bone, and one that ought to have been picked clean by now, Celia thought indignantly. However, since she was quite anxious to satisfy herself on the subject of Lady Laura and would satisfy herself if her brother invited her to ride with them, she said merely, "You will remember that I was only just wed myself."

Her brother gave her a long, measuring glance before saying obliquely, "Very well. And will you be joining us in the park, then?"

"I will be delighted," his sister said enthusiastically.

Laura, riding Charity, her spirited chestnut mare, and with Lady Howard close at her side mounted on Fraxinella, a dun mare called after a well-known racehorse but with a deliberate disposition that quite belied her name, listened impatiently to her chaperone's adjurations concerning the inadvisability of cantering along these paths.

"You will not wish to be thought mannish," her ladyship concluded.

"Might I not at least suit my pace to his?" Laura demanded disappointedly.

"I suggest that you attempt no more than a decorous trot." Lady Howard said after a moment given over to considering her charge's question.

With considerable difficulty Laura refrained from asking Lady Howard how one might manage to be decorous on horseback. Besides, as she watched her chaperone guide her horse along the bridle path, she realized that she had before her a more than adequate example. It was truly amazing how her mentor managed to take the joy out of every occasion at which she was present. In fact, she seemed to carry her own rain cloud with her—for directly she had arrived at the stables, a gray-edged cloud had drifted over the sun. More clouds were presently appearing, she noted, and she hoped devoutly that it would not rain. Still, she thought bitterly, that might be well within Lady Howard's province too.

Her unhappy thoughts were scattered as two riders suddenly appeared in the distance. As they drew nearer, Laura saw Lord Marne in the lead and mounted on a magnificent black stallion. Behind him was a very lovely young woman riding a chestnut gelding. She was wearing a brown habit that was almost the same color as her eyes. As she and his lordship came closer, an agonizing Laura was relieved to find a strong family resemblance between the pair. Before she could come to any more conclusions, they had ridden up and she must control a suddenly fractious Charity, while being introduced to Lady Belmore, his lordship's sister.

Having finally subdued Charity, Laura looked up to find Lord Marne beside her. "G-good afternoon, my l-lord," she stuttered, and agonized again over having stuttered, and agonized yet again as she realized she had already exchanged that greeting with him.

"Good afternoon, Lady Laura," he said cordially. "May I congratulate you on your admirable control of your mount?"

"I thank you. Poor Charity gets rattled ever so often," Laura explained, feeling rattled herself as she found it necessary to rein Charity in again, thus needing to reluctantly divide her attention between his lordship and her steed.

"I find that the weather often has a less than salubrious effect on these spirited horses." He glanced upward at a sky that was becoming more overcast by the minute. "I awoke to sunshine," he continued, "but it seems as if Apollo's chariot is being overtaken by Jove."

"Oh, dear, I hope not. I have been so looking forward to . . ." Laura reddened. "I mean . . ."

"I hope that you meant you had been looking forward to our ride," Lord Marne said. "I know I have." He added, "Shall we go on ahead and hope that we are not driven back by the elements? Perhaps we might even race?"

"Oh, I should like that!" Laura exclaimed enthusiastically. Then, mindful of Lady Howard, she added. "Only . . ."

"Only what?" he demanded. "This path will lead us to within a sight of the Serpentine. The first one who sees it will win the race. Come . . ." He urged his horse forward.

He was not even going to give her a handicap, Laura realized joyfully as she, in turn, urged Charity onward. Lord Marne was a few paces ahead and unmindful of a warning cry from Lady Howard. Laura clicked her tongue at Charity and in another few minutes had outdistanced his lordship. He, of course, did not remain passively behind. He was ahead of her in another few moments, his triumphant laughter inciting her to a further burst of speed.

Laura was in sight of a shimmering length of blue behind the sheltering trees, and the word *Serpentine* was gleefully forming on her lips when, with a searing flash of lightning and an ominous roll of thunder, the skies opened to allow the descent of a veritable deluge. With an actual scream of fright, Charity tossed her rider into a thicket and, turning tail, fled back in the direction of the stables.

"You will get no sympathy from *me,*" Lady Roswell said icily as she stood just inside the door of Laura's chamber, where the latter lay on a pile of pillows. "You promised Lady Howard that you would not race."

"I . . . I did not intend to race," Laura moaned. "He suggested it."

"I cannot believe that," Lady Roswell responded sharply.

"Well, he did, Mama." Laura wished strongly that her mother would leave and allow her to suffer in peace. She had fallen amid thorns and these had not only penetrated into her riding habit, they also had pierced portions of her nether parts. That was what was hurting her the most—the fact that Lord Marne, while extracting her from the thicket, had necessarily viewed those same parts. Her only hope was that they had not really registered on him as, looking extremely concerned and unmindful of the pelting rain, he had carefully pulled the thorny branches away and then, placing her on his saddlebow, had ridden back to the stables.

She had read a great deal about gallant knights placing distressed damsels before them on their saddlebows—but those damsels had invariably been slim, fairylike maidens with glowing golden locks, and they had generally assumed that particular perch in clement weather. They had certainly not been held against a gallant quite as soggy as the maiden he had rescued and with hands, scratched and bleeding from dealing with the thicket. Furthermore his dark, waving hair, probably concealed by a helmet in those days, was not lying wetly across his forehead, and above all, such a gallant would not have been shaking with laughter for which he apologized over and over again, only to continue laughing.

"You," her mother said coldly, "were determined to show him your prowess in the saddle. Well, my dear Laura, you have shown him. Pride goeth before a fall and never was a saying more true . . ." She paused at a tap on the door. "Yes?" she asked loudly and crossly as she opened the portal.

Thomas, one of the footmen, said, "There's a letter come for you, Lady Roswell. It was just brought 'ere." He held out a silver tray on which reposed an envelope.

Lady Roswell took the envelope. "Thank you, Thomas," she said in less pejorative accents. "You may go." As the door closed behind the footman, Lady Roswell, glancing at the envelope, said, "It is from Lord Marne. Very possibly he wishes to clear you of blame for your folly this afternoon, and take it upon himself. He is the very soul of courtesy. What a pity that we will probably see him no more."

A sob escaped Laura. "He did not seem angry . . . he was only s-sorry that my horse threw me."

Lady Roswell, her lips pressed together in a thin line of disapproval, opened the envelope. Taking out a folded sheet of paper, she opened it so impatiently that she tore off a corner. Then, as she perused it, she let it drop to the floor as she exclaimed, "Good God!"

"What is it, Mama?" Laura sat up and then sank back with a groan as she was assailed by aches and pains in all portions of her anatomy.

Lady Roswell had retrieved the letter, and she read it yet again. "The man is mad!" she cried.

"I . . . I do not understand you, Mama! What does he say?" Laura demanded.

"He says that . . . that . . ." Lady Roswell gasped, and then suddenly sat down on a nearby chair as if her legs had just collapsed beneath her.

"Mama!" Laura exclaimed. "You . . . you have turned white. Do you need the hartshorn? What is it? Please t-tell me!"

"Lord Marne wishes . . . he . . . he wishes to . . . to marry you, Laura," Lady Roswell said in faint, unbelieving tones. "As . . . as soon as you have r-recovered." She held the letter up. "It . . . it is a formal offer. I never . . . I never thought such a thing would ever happen."

Laura paid no attention to her mother's unflattering reception of news that was filling her with a most unfamiliar emotion. It was only after it had persisted for some little time that she was able to define it as ecstasy.

THREE

LADY BELMORE PACED UP AND DOWN the well-furnished library that lay on the second floor of her brother's London house. Her dark eyes were twin mirrors of disapproval. "But you cannot marry a young woman merely because she amuses you, Eric. You do not love her!"

Lord Marne said, "She is intelligent and she needs rescuing."

"Rescuing?" she echoed. "From whom or what?"

"From her chaperone," he replied, becoming more obscure by the moment, his exasperated sister thought.

"Do you know what the word *rescue* means to me?" she demanded.

"No, you will have to explain your meaning." He smiled.

"I see Andromeda chained to a rock . . . I see dragons and knights at arms and beautiful maidens. Lady Laura is neither a beautiful maiden, nor is she surrounded by dragons—so why are you donning knight-errant armor?"

"Dragons may come in many shapes, Celia," he said gravely. "Unless I am deeply mistaken, Laura's dragons are named Lady Howard and Lady Roswell . . . both of them keep her from being herself. I am becoming rather fond of her."

"But she is so . . . so . . ."

As she paused, searching for a proper adjective, he said quickly, "So . . . what? You cannot tell me that she is not well born. Her family tree stretches back just as far as our own. She has a large dowry. She might not be beautiful, she is far too heavy, but she is pleasant company and she is certainly undemanding."

"You are not in love with her, not in the least," she accused.

His smile vanished. "Am I supposed to be in love with her? How many marriages among us are based on love?"

"Mine," his sister responded promptly. "And you once said that nothing would ever make you . . ." She paused as he held up a hand.

"Anything I once said is to be ignored and forgotten. I married for love *once*. Such a feeling will not come to me again. Lady Laura is well connected, very well. She is rich. I cannot understand why we are having this discussion. I thought you would be delighted by my decision."

She was silent, gazing at him rather sadly. Then she said slowly, "I am not delighted by it, Eric, dearest. We are having this discussion because I happen to believe that a man of your temperament—*you*, Eric,—needs to be in love." Celia's eyes filled with tears. "Supposing after you are wed you should meet someone you do love?"

He said stubbornly, "Lightning never strikes twice in the same place. Would you have me withdraw my offer because for once in my life I am being extremely practical? I could not withdraw it, Celia, my dear, even were I to be assailed by second thoughts. I would not hurt that poor child. She has already been hurt too much by well-intentioned persons who, as far as I can see, do not take her feelings into account. She is not without feelings, Celia."

"He is marrying that girl out of *kindness,*" Celia told her husband that night. "Poor Eric, oh, I do so loathe that creature!"

Her husband regarded her with mild surprise. "I thought you rather like her."

"Whatever gave you that impression?" Celia demanded hotly. "In spite of the poor baby, I was not at all sorry when she died, that is the truth of it."

"Oh, you were speaking about his wife," Lord Belmore said.

"Whom did you think I meant?" she demanded edgily.

"I beg your pardon, my love. I had the impression you were speaking about Lady Laura."

"Oh, no, I am only sorry for her, poor thing. I think she is quite madly in love with Eric, and he has done nothing to discourage her, more's the pity."

"Why should he, since he is planning to marry her?" Lord Belmore stared at her confusedly.

"Can you not guess?" she asked challengingly.

"No, I must admit that it is a conundrum that escapes me. You are not making very much sense, my dear."

"I am making perfect sense," she said stubbornly.

Unknowingly Lady Roswell shared some of Celia's opinions, and these she felt incumbent upon herself to pass on to Laura even though the plans for the wedding, due to take place at St. James's Church in mid-June, were proceeding at a most satisfactory pace. She chose a time when Laura, flushed and happy from her first visit to St. Bartholomew's Fair in company with her fiancé, was describing its wonders.

"He is kind," Lady Roswell commented. "I think you will deal together very well. It is really the very best sort of a marriage. I think it much more important to be friends with the man you marry. I am pleased that you appear to be acquainted with the fact that he is not madly in love with you."

The pleasure of the afternoon was suddenly abated. Laura was aware that Lord Marne was not madly in love with her. She knew that he was more friendly than loverlike. She had had plenty of opportunity to witness husbands who were loverlike. Julia's lord treated her as if she were a piece of rare porcelain. His eyes glowed when she came into a room. He seemed to be speaking with the rest of the family, but actually he hardly ever heard what was being said to him. His eyes were on Julia, his thoughts were fixed on her—she was his life! Margaret's husband was less overt, but that he adored her was unmistakable. As for herself, she wished strongly that she might refute what her mother believed to be "well-meant" advice, which, in this case, was merely stating the obvious.

Unfortunately one did have to be realistic, and her grandmother had felt it incumbent upon herself to tell Laura about the late Lady Marne and her tragic death— an account that differed very little from those she had already heard on that never to be forgotten second visit to Almack's, when *he* had unaccountably asked her to dance. The countess had concluded a considerably more detailed version of the tale with the words, "He must have an heir."

"He must have an heir," Lady Roswell said.

Laura, startled, looked at her mother, realizing that she had not heard much of what she had been saying. Obviously it must not have differed in content from her grandmother's comments. She said, "Yes, I know. I will try to be a good wife to him, Mama—and now, if you will excuse me?"

"Of course, my dear," Lady Roswell said. Then, obviously feeling that something more should be added, she continued, "I am sure he is becoming fond of you."

"He is very pleasant, Mama," Laura said. "Will you excuse me? I must change my clothes."

"Yes, dear, of course. And do not forget that you are due at the theater tonight—Sir John and Lady Caldwell. Old friends."

"From Norwich. Yes, I remember, Mama." Laura hurried out of the room and, arriving in her own

chamber, told herself strongly that she must not weep.
She must needs be realistic and not long for what he
could not give her. She did enjoy his company. She had
enjoyed it greatly that afternoon. They had watched a
balloon ascension. They had laughed at the antics of a
trained pig, and they had been similarly disgusted at a
sideshow exhibit, the pig-faced woman. They had agreed
that she ought not to be put on display for crowds to
gawk at and discuss with horror or amusement as if she
were bereft of feelings. Expressing a mutual distaste, they
had hurried out, and then he had waltzed with her on a
little platform with other couples and afterward treated
her to a lemon ice.

Obviously he enjoyed being with her, but he seemed
more like an older brother than a lover, and Laura was
quite aware that there were portions of his mind that
would unlock to no verbal key. That was only too
apparent in the occasional brooding sadness that appeared in his eyes when she guessed something reminded
him of his late wife and lost love.

She could not be jealous of her and should not be. Poor
Christina had died so young, and oddly enough, despite
her own burgeoning happiness, she wished that the lady
had not died. She was generous enough to resent it when
Lady Celia spoke about her in the most disparaging
terms. The countess, too, had aroused her ire when she
said sharply, "The late Lady Marne was a featherbrain,
and selfish to the bone. Had she lived a little longer, her
husband would have found it out, I can assure you, my
dear Laura. It is extremely unfortunate that he did not.
She was not born to be idolized, much less canonized.

Despite her pity for the late Christina, Laura did think
about her conversation with her mother off and on
during the play that night, and once she was home again,
she had needed to make a strong effort to keep from
crying herself to sleep. However, the next morning, she
was more philosophical, and fortunately, in the days that
followed, she had little time to dwell on her bridegroom's

late wife. Her days were spent in visits to the mantua maker's where, in addition to the fittings for her wedding gown, she was having a whole new wardrobe made. It would consist of stylish ensembles that a maid-into-matron might wear, and which, her mother said, suited her better than her demure muslins. While this was not precisely a compliment, it did raise spirits that occasionally flagged when she thought of the willowy figure of the late Lady Marne. Then there was the need to meet with relatives that she had not seen in years but who came into London from such distant places as Edinburgh, Yorkshire, and the Isle of Man. They came bearing gifts she must needs acknowledge. Other relations wrote sending gifts which again required notes. These her mother composed for Laura to copy.

Most important was, of course, her wedding gown, which, unfortunately, must needs be white rather than the blue or violet that would have lent its hue to her eyes. However, for the last three years, white and only white was de rigueur for wedding gowns, and as Laura was only too aware, she would look twice her size in white. She was to wear the veil, lacy and long, which had been passed down by her grandmother. It would, unfortunately, conceal her hair—the color of which pleased her bridegroom, as he had told her more than once. He would not be seeing her hair. He would only be seeing her full face, flushed pink, she feared, by excitement.

She had begged Mrs. Bell to find a way to make her appear less gigantic in white, and the lady had obliged with a panel of cream-colored lace down the front, which, she insisted, would create the illusion of slimness. Laura was doubtful about that, but since she dared not challenge the mantua maker's decisions, she could only hope for the best and, while she was hoping, pray that Julia would remain in Land's End, which lay some two hundred and ninety miles from London and where her husband had an estate to which he had insisted they go after one of their many quarrels. As usual, it had revolved around the attentions of one Lord Carleton, whom Lord Ludlow had accused his wife of encouraging. Were Julia to insist on taking the long journey to London, she must easily outshine everyone present— including the bride or, rather, especially the bride. For perhaps the millionth time Laura wished that she had more in common with her sister than the timber of her voice, which, everyone said, was amazingly similar.

As the day drew nearer, Laura was comforted by the fact that Julia had not arrived. It was wrong to feel as she did about her sister, but all too often she had been the brunt of Julia's pointed remarks concerning her size. Her sister had also lectured her on the dangers of becoming a bluestocking because of her copious reading. In vain, Laura had protested that she did not write.

"Writing, my dear Laura, will be the next step. I can see you sitting at a desk, your fingers ink-stained and spectacles on the end of your nose—and I can see myself sending you a pair of blue stockings."

That Julia had not forgotten that threat was apparent when, in the note accompanying the handsome silver candelabra she had sent as a wedding gift, there was a note wishing her well and, in the postscript, a line stating, "I could not find any blue stockings in all of Land's End."

Lord Marne had wanted to know the meaning of that note and had laughed when she explained, saying lightly that he was looking forward to meeting Julia. It had been wrong to feel so strong a stab of jealousy, and she was extremely glad that he could not read her mind. Yet it was on Julia that Laura was dwelling when she opened her eyes very early on the morning of June 9, 1816, her wedding day.

A note sent by messenger had arrived the previous evening. The envelope had borne Julia's careless black scrawl. After all, by dint of traveling night and day, she would be present at her sister's wedding even if in an unofficial capacity, by which she meant, not as a bridesmaid. Lady Roswell had been delighted, speaking with uncharacteristic sentimentality about all her "chicks" being under one roof—save for her son, at present in India.

"Oh, dear," Laura murmured unhappily. "Let her coach break down on the road . . . let a sudden storm rise, unlikely in June, but possible." Then common sense took over. It was foolish to worry about Julia—it was her wedding day.

It was also a day that passed like a dream. It seemed to Laura that scarcely had she opened her eyes than she was garbed in her white gown, which, in her mirror, made her look as she had feared—twice her size. Then she was in the coach, her tearful mother murmuring that she was losing the last of her babies, quite as if she were not absolutely ecstatic over having married her youngest and least prepossessing daughter to a rich, handsome bridegroom of impeccable lineage, a triumph neither Margaret nor Julia had achieved.

Laura was never quite sure how she came to be standing at the back of the church with her bridesmaids, nor how she was suddenly proceeding slowly up the aisle to the altar, where the minister stood ready to unite her with the tall, handsome stranger waiting for her, the unsmiling stranger who had stared at her as if she were equally strange to him. Indeed, it had seemed to Laura that rather than looking at her, Lord Marne's gaze was turned inward. However, when it came to the responses, which she spoke hesitantly, his had been firm, even if voiced in a lower tone than was generally his wont.

Then the minister was blessing them and they were hurrying up the aisle to the open doors. They came out of the church to crowds of interested spectators. Subsequently they were helped into a coach and driven to the reception given by Lady Roswell, this after a three-day argument with the countess, who had wanted it to take place at her mansion. However, a mother who has so creditably disposed of three daughters, and with the last and least of them making by far the most influential marriage, was not to be stared down and out-argued by her mother-in-law!

Stepping over the threshold of her mother's house symbolically for the last time, Laura still felt as if she were dreaming. Oddly enough, uppermost in her mind was the fact that despite her ominous letter, Julia had not been present in the church. Evidently her prayers had been answered. Her sister must have been delayed on the road! That was really all she needed to complete her happiness, she realized, and immediately castigated herself for a most unsisterly thought.

Meanwhile she was automatically nodding and smiling and thanking her bridesmaids and others for their good wishes, and at the same time longing to find a nook where she could sit and watch the handsome people at the reception, as she usually did, without participating, which was much more comfortable, really. Now, however, she was surrounded by her bridesmaids, none of whom she knew very well. They were daughters of family friends for the most part, and from their expressions some of them were more surprised than elated at her good fortune. However, they were all wishing her happy and, of course, she could not slip away. She looked for her bridegroom and was amazed to find him at her side. A glance at his face showed her that he was smiling as congratulations were spoken. Then, suddenly, his gaze grew fixed and he stiffened.

"Laura, Laura, my dearest, oh, I was so dreadfully afraid that we would miss the reception!" Julia caroled. She threw her arms around her sister and kissed her on the cheek. "Congratulations, my dearest."

Laura fastened dazed eyes on Julia, who, on drawing back, was found to be wearing a blue gown that matched her great eyes. Her golden hair clustered about her lovely face, and as usual, she was as slim as a fairy. Then, on turning to the bridegroom, she stared up at him in an amazement that widened her eyes and, for a split second, her mouth as well.

Laura said, "E-Eric," his name unfamiliar to her tongue. "My sister Julia."

He bowed over Julia's hand. "Your servant, ma'am," he murmured.

"But I am delighted." Julia seemed to be having difficulty in speaking, for she did not offer any further congratulations.

Then others closed in on the newly wedded pair, and Julia vaguely acknowledged the greetings she was receiving from friends she had not seen in months—not since being, in effect, exiled to the far end of Cornwall. She wished that she might speak to her mother, but a glance around the room showed her Lady Roswell surrounded by other well-wishers. Consequently she could not ask her how it happened that Laura, large and clumsy, looking twice her size in white, could have married so well—an earl, a dashing young earl and so handsome that he might almost be called beautiful and, judging from his interested reaction on meeting herself, not in love with the chit, either. Indeed, how could he be? Frederick had told her that he knew the bridegroom at Cambridge, she suddenly remembered.

She tried to remember what else he had said and looked around for her husband. She found him speaking to the groom and smiling at Laura, whom he had always liked for reasons she never had been able to understand. Though one was supposed to love a sister, Julia had always found Laura singularly difficult to love or, for that matter, even to like! She was such a lump! And now this lump, this fat, clumsy creature who was practically bursting out of her gown, had made the match of the season, and in her first season, too—which was a miracle, indeed. Reasons flew into her head and were summarily dismissed. Though Laura did appear very large in that unbecoming gown with the lace panel down the front that made her look even wider in the hips, she was positive that Lord Marne never would have gotten her sister with child!

"It is amazing, is it not?" someone commented.

Julia turned to find Lady Turnbull, an old friend whom she had known in school. She was recently wed to Sir Roderick Turnbull, not a brilliant match to be sure but one based on love, as hers had been, she had believed— for who would have expected Frederick to be such a bear! She said, "Althea, my dear, yes, I do find it amazing, Laura of all people."

"It has been the talk of the town," Althea murmured. "She is certainly nothing like his first wife."

"Oh, has he been married before?" Julia asked interestedly. "Mama failed to tell me that. And what was *she* like, his first wife?"

"The most utterly beautiful creature, my dear. They married at the beginning of her first season . . . It seems to be a habit with him. This is Laura's first season, is it not?"

"Yes." Julia nodded, adding impatiently, "Tell me more about him. I have heard nothing."

"How might you in Cornwall? How do you bear it, my dear? It is the very end of the earth!"

"Oh, it has its beauties," Julia assured her, thoroughly disliking her erstwhile friend for implications she could not refute. "You were telling me about Lord Marne's first wife. He must have been very young when he married."

"He was twenty-one and she was seventeen. They were divinely happy, entirely wrapped up in each other, and living in the country."

"They lived entirely in the country?" Julia regarded her wide-eyed.

"Entirely. The town knew them no more for three or four years, I am not quite sure the length of time. Then she died in childbed two years ago."

"Oh, dear, how tragic," Julia murmured.

"Yes, it was tragic. He fell into the deepest melancholy. His sister Celia, a friend of mine, told me that they feared he might take his own life . . . and I believe he is still affected, but family pressures, you understand. He is the last of his line and there must be an heir."

"Oh, of course." Julia nodded.

Althea regarded her thoughtfully. "Do you know, Julia, my dear, poor Christina looked a great deal like you?"

"Christina being, of course, his late wife?" Julia questioned. As her friend nodded, she felt singularly cheered by news that could not be discounted as mere gossip. Certainly it explained Laura's remarkable marriage, and it also explained the bridegroom's fixed stare at her.

Not for the first time Julia wished that she had not rushed so gladly into marriage with Frederick, a mere viscount. She had loved him, or rather she had thought she loved him. Still, who could have known that he would prove so very jealous over the most trifling matters? She looked at Laura, red-faced and beaming, as she stood next to that singularly handsome young man. He was not beaming. Indeed, he was looking sober and meeting his eye; she smiled warmly at him, mentally welcoming him into the family. She was extremely pleased to receive an answering smile, and even more pleased when that smile faded as Laura looked up to say something to him. Though Julia was not very familiar with the Bible, it seemed to her that some king had been strongly impressed and at the same time depressed when he had seen some handwriting on the wall of his palace. She, herself, seemed to see much the same thing magically appearing on her mother's striped wallpaper, but it did not depress her in the least!

The wedding feast took place at three in the afternoon, so that the newly wedded couple could begin the first leg of their journey to Somerset before sundown. The bridegroom's castle was located near the historic town of Chard, though according to Lord Marne, his home was less a castle than a manor house, the latter rising as had many other houses after the depredations of the Civil War.

"That it is still called Marne Castle is out of respect to its historic past rather than to its more mundane present," Laura remembered him telling her.

"Knights and cavaliers rode out of its storied gates,

and country gentlemen rode back in later years." He had spoken rather wryly, as if, indeed, he regretted the armor and the banners, the spears and the war machines, though why that occurred to her, she did not know. She was thinking about that conversation as her excited new abigail, Lucy Browne, arrayed her in her going-away gown, which, thanks be to heaven, was not white but a muted blue silk that complimented her eyes and her coloring.

Elaine Walwyn, one of the girls she had known from her brief year at a private school in Bath, was helping Laura dress, and so was Marina Fitzwilliam, a friend from home. They were both excited and at the same time surprised that she was marrying so handsome and well connected a young man, Laura knew. She could not blame them for that. She had read varying degrees of that same surprise on the faces of many wedding guests. However, it had been most obvious when Julia, who had just now entered her chamber, had come to speak to herself and Lord Marne, whom she must remember to think about as Eric, her husband! It was early to adjust her thinking, and she could not help believing that she was in a dream from which she must soon awaken.

Why was Julia here at this moment? she wondered. Margaret was directing Lucy as to what she must take on the journey. Julia, however, had not come to help her. That was not her way. Furthermore, the smile with which she had greeted her below was missing. For reasons she could not quite explain, Laura braced herself as Julia reached her side. Still, she managed to say politely, if not truthfully, "I am pleased that you were able to come to my reception, Julia."

"I am pleased that we were able to reach London in time," Julia responded. "You are fortunate, indeed, Laura."

"I know I am," Laura said simply, thinking that her sister's eyes were as cold as twin pieces of ice. In fact, she had an almost overwhelming urge to hold up two fingers as she had seen old Janet do when she was warding off what she termed "the evil eye." Julia was staring at her as if she actually hated her.

She said, however, "I do wish you well, and one day I hope you will invite me to your home in Somerset—such a lovely part of the country."

"We will certainly do so," Laura said warmly now, her happiness returning with the delightfully allowable substitution of *we* for *I*. And then she wished that she had not made that particular promise, or at least she wished she had not expressed it in quite that way, for she received another narrowed glance as Julia responded, "I will remember that, my dear." Then she leaned forward and kissed Laura on both cheeks before hurrying out of the room.

Almost unthinkingly Laura put both hands to her cheeks, feeling, indeed, as if rather than receiving kisses they had been stung by a pair of furious bees.

"How very beautiful your sister is," Elaine murmured.

Margaret, who was close at hand, murmured, "Beauty is as beauty does." She bent a compassionate look on Laura, and moving nearer, she said, "Julia is Julia, but Frederick has told me that they are returning to Cornwall within the week."

Laura looked at her older sister in surprise. "You noticed?" She would have gone on, but Margaret interrupted her quickly. "You must not let her spoil your day, my dear. And . . ." But whatever else she might have said fell into silence as the countess, with Jane behind her, entered the room.

"Ah, my dear Laura." Her grandmother looked up at her. "You must always wear blue, must she not, Jane?"

"Aye, your ladyship," Jane said. Her eyes, gray and deep-set, lingered on Laura's face.

"Jane counts herself the harbinger of your happiness, my dear." The countess stood on tiptoe to kiss Laura's cheek. "You are such a giantess—but your husband is taller yet. My felicitations, my dearest. Jane, you must admit, has outdone herself."

"She has." Laura, looking into the ancient abigail's

hooded gray eyes, was, as usual, unnerved by their intensity. "I do thank you, Jane."

"I am not to be thanked," the old woman said in a low voice. "I tell what I see, and I see you happy . . . in time."

It was an odd thing for her to say. Implicit in her comment—or was it a prediction?—was delay, Laura thought, and hoped devoutly that she was wrong.

"Of course she will be happy, you silly old woman," the countess said briskly. "How could she not be happy, Jane? Lord Marne is a handsome, charming young man, and he is also intelligent. You are very fortunate, my dear."

"And so is he . . ." Jane murmured.

"What?" The countess frowned. "But of course they are both fortunate."

"Yes . . . both." Jane nodded.

Having had her say or, rather, having done her duty by her granddaughter, the countess whirled out of the chamber, followed by Jane, moving slowly, as usual. As she reached the door she glanced back over her shoulder and nodded at Laura, her expression enigmatic and, to Laura's mind, rather grim. Furthermore, those of her words that remained longest in her thoughts were only two. "In time."

As Laura came down the stairs there was a group of people waiting for her on the first floor and looking up expectantly. However, Eric was not among them. He was near the door and he was not looking in his bride's direction. He could not, for Julia was speaking to him, smiling provocatively up at him and receiving a warm smile in return from one who had eyes for none other. It seemed to Laura as if everyone were suddenly looking at the pair by the door and, in consequence, were she to throw her bouquet, there would be no one to catch it, and it must needs remain unclaimed on the stairs. Yet it was the custom, and certainly she must throw it.

"Does no one . . ." she began, but her voice faded into silence as Julia stood on tiptoe to kiss the bridegroom's cheek and to cry warmly, "For luck, my dear brother-in-law."

The bouquet dropped from Laura's suddenly nerveless fingers and fell on the stairs where Lady Celia hastily retrieved it as Laura reached the bottom of the stairs and Lord Marne, hurriedly parting from Julia, came to put an arm around his wife's waist and to say in surprise, "But you are shivering, my dear. Surely you are not cold."

She looked upward and, meeting his eyes, read concern in them. "I . . . I dropped my bouquet. I hope it is not an ill omen," she said, and then tried to laugh. "But that is a foolish thing to say, is it not?"

"It is, my dear, and certainly it is not an ill omen," Lady Celia said behind them. She returned the flowers to Laura. "Here," she added, "you must throw it, and we will see whom the next bride will be!"

"Yes," the bridesmaids chorused. "Come, Laura!"

Feeling oddly confused, Laura obeyed, flinging the bouquet high, higher, than she had intended so that it sailed over the extended hands of her bridesmaids and the wedding guests to fall toward Julia, who made no effort to retrieve it. Instead, she merely scooped it up from the floor once it had fallen at her feet.

"You should have caught it, Julia." Her mother frowned at her.

"But"—Julia laughed lightly—"I am married already, am I not?"

"I think we must go." Lord Marne smiled at Laura and slipped his arm around her waist. "We have a ways to go before sunset." He escorted her quickly through the assembled wedding guests. Their good wishes rang in her ears, and at the door, her mother kissed her farewell. Then they were on their way to the waiting coach, and Julia must needs remain behind. Laura, glancing back over her shoulder, failed to glimpse her sister and was glad of that.

FOUR

A SHOWER OF rice followed Laura and her bridegroom into the well-sprung traveling coach with Lord Marne's family crest of a lion rampant in gold on a dark green door. Her abigail and his valet rode in another large coach on which was strapped Laura's trunk and his lordship's portmanteau. There were four outriders, and there was also a fine saddle horse, which, Eric had told Laura, he intended to ride for part of the way. Since it would take something under three days to reach their destination, they were booked into two inns.

As they rolled down the street, Laura, sitting with one hand clutching the strap by the window, found herself suddenly tongue-tied, while Eric, sitting near the other window, was similarly silent. He was not usually so constrained, Laura thought. And of course, she hastily reminded herself, neither was she. In the days before this one, he had always had plenty to say about where they would be going, whether it was to look at the jewels in the Tower of London or to visit the exhibits at the British Museum. She wondered what he was thinking—she also wondered what might lie ahead. They would reach the first inn by seven or eight that evening, she had been told. Then, as the silence grew oppressive, she said shyly, "I expect . . ." and paused, for he had cleared his throat as if he were about to speak.

They looked at each other and laughed nervously. "You were about to say, my dear?" he inquired.

Laura noted that he was not looking directly at her. Indeed, it seemed as if his gaze were fixed upon a spot over her head. "I . . . do not remember. What were you about to say, E-Eric?"

"I thought I would tell you a little about the road over which we will be traveling. I do not believe you have been to this part of Somerset."

"I have not done much traveling at all," she said.

"You have never been on the Continent?"

"No." She forbore to mention that he had asked her that once before. "I know you have," she said, by way of a gentle reminder.

"Yes, I have been to Paris."

"It must be a beautiful city."

"Yes, it is, very." Then he added abruptly, "Your sister Julia . . ."

A pulse rose in Laura's throat and pounded there. "Yes?"

"She lives in Cornwall?"

"Yes, in Land's End. That is where Frederick's estate is located. Though I must say that she much prefers London." Then other words rose in her throat, demanding utterance. She said, albeit reluctantly, "Julia is very beautiful, is she not?"

"Yes." He nodded. "Very."

She wished that he had not been in such haste to agree, but how could he not? "Julia," she continued bravely, "is the beauty of the family. The year she came out, she was voted an Incomparable by Beau Brummel and others at White's. The poor Beau, I do feel sorry for him, do you not?" she added, in hopes that she might change the subject.

"Yes," he said gravely, "there will be many who will miss him, but one does make a great mistake to depend upon the favor of princes . . . and an even greater mistake to insult them." He was silent a moment, then, as if he could not help himself, he continued, "Your sister was married her first season?"

"Yes, that was five years ago."

He regarded her in surprise. "You will not be telling me that she is already in her twenties!"

"Oh, yes," Laura said with a melancholy satisfaction. "Julia will be twenty-four in October. Though certainly she does not appear that old."

"No, I certainly never would have thought so," he agreed. "Does she have any children?"

"Not as yet. It has been a great disappointment to her and to her husband," Laura explained, and felt her face grow hot as she remembered the main reason she was here in this coach and with Lord Marne's wide gold ring on the requisite finger.

"He must have an heir, my dear," her mother and her grandmother had emphasized.

"Many young women do not have children until later in life," Eric said.

"I expect they do not." Laura nodded. "Though my brother Geoffrey was born less than a year after Mama was married."

"How old is your brother?"

"He will be thirty in August. Margaret is two years younger, and Julia, as I told you. No one really expected me."

"No, you are six years younger than Julia—a child, really."

"I do not feel a child," Laura said defensively. "I am turned eighteen."

"Yes, I do know that," he said teasingly. "I know all about you, Laura." Moving closer to her, he kissed her lightly on the cheek.

In that moment it seemed to Laura that a whole bevy of shadows hovering in her mind flew out, losing themselves in the sky. She smiled up at him. "Do you know,

E-Eric, I am very happy," she murmured.

He slipped his arm around her shoulders. "We must see that you continue that way, my dear."

She wished that he might have answered that he, too, was happy, but perhaps that is what he had implied when his arm had tightened around her shoulders. She thrilled to the sensation of his closeness.

It was nearly eight and the sun a dark streak of red on the western horizon when they reached the King's Rest, a large coaching inn outside of Reading. Built around a vast, cobblestoned courtyard and with all its chambers on the second floor, the inn was welcome indeed to Laura. Though the coach was well sprung and the going reasonably smooth, there had been some rough stretches of road, resulting in a need to clutch the strap at her side to keep from being thrown to the floor. Furthermore, by eight, the excitement of the day had diminished, and she was feeling unexpectedly weary. Eric, too, looked tired, and the chamber into which an obsequious innkeeper had showed them was a very welcome sight. Once the innkeeper had bowed himself out promising to send up the small repast Eric had requested, Laura sank down in a wing chair.

"Oh." She sighed. "This is comfortable, and it is also stationary!"

"Coach travel can be strenuous, my dear." Eric smiled at her. "I think we need not rise too early tomorrow morning."

"T-that would be n-nice if it were not necessary," Laura stuttered, belatedly struck by the realization that she and her husband were alone in the chamber.

He said, "I am glad you agree." Staring down at her, he added, "My love, I think that . . . that given the exigencies of road travel, it were better if we made use of separate rooms until we reach our destination."

Casting a glance around the room, Laura suddenly noticed that there were two doors opening off this chamber. She said, "As you wish, Eric," and was caught between relief and confusion as she remembered certain confidences embarrassedly vouchsafed by her mother concerning her wedding night.

He regarded her anxiously. "You will not mind . . . waiting, then?"

"No, of course not," she assured him. "It has been a very wearisome day."

"Indeed it has," he agreed, and bent to kiss her, his lips brushing her mouth. "You are a dear girl," he added gratefully.

Later, after a repast Laura had hardly touched, being, as she explained to Eric, too tired to eat, she went to bed. Lucy, hovering about her, looked as if she wanted to say something, but on opening her mouth, she closed it. Finally, on bidding her mistress a constrained good night, she hurried out of the room, leaving Laura with the feeling of a spate of soundless comments hovering in the air behind her. There was, of course, no reason for her to weep into her pillow, and her tears were of short duration. It *had* been a tiring day, tiring and trying, and might have been considerably less so had her sister Julia been delayed on the road.

In his own chamber, Eric, too, lay awake, guiltily aware that he should not be reveling in the wide expanse of mattress he was not sharing with anyone. Yet on flinging his arms out and drawing them back slowly to his sides, he was very glad that they had met with no impediment to a freedom he had experienced, if not enjoyed, for two years. He was enjoying it now, and he was also bitterly regretting having yielded to family pressure.

Despite his fondness for Laura—and he was *fond* of her, he assured himself—there was the vibrant memory of Christina, and once more he was assailed by the image that had haunted him off and on through the hours it had taken to reach the inn. Julia! Julia, who so resembled Christina and who was alive and infinitely desirable! To think of her was to want her, and he did not believe himself mistaken when he had read the same longing in her eyes, those incredibly beautiful violet eyes!

In the few moments during which they had been able to speak to each other, he had come to the belated realization that he had been far too willing to accede to the wishes of his aunt and his sister. He should have waited!

"Waited for whom?" he murmured. "Another Julia?"

There could be no other, he knew, and he was married. She, too, was married, but unhappily, as unhappily as himself, he realized with a shock, and what was he to do about that? He could seek an annulment—but he could not hurt poor Laura, he decided wretchedly. It was not her fault that her sister was so much more beautiful than herself, so infinitely more desirable, and who looked at him with Christina's eyes! She also possessed his late love's way of making him almost agonizingly aware of herself—without so much as touching him! In common with Christina, Julia touched him—figuratively holding him in her arms and making him ache with longing for her. Furthermore, Julia had made him feel that she shared his passion. Indeed, when she had stood on tiptoe and let her lips brush his cheek, it had been all he could do not to embrace her before all the wedding guests! He was quite sure that Julia's failure to catch Laura's bouquet was her way of showing him just what she did feel for him.

"Oh, God, God, God, what am I going to do?" He groaned. "I must see her again. Yet how?"

There was no answer to that painful question. He could not leave the inn as he would like to do, leave his unwanted bride behind, leave his responsibilities behind and ride to Cornwall. He had to consider Laura when, at this particular moment, he almost hated her for needing him as much as he was sure she did.

Julia had a husband, too, he reminded himself, but again, without resorting to speech, she had let him know that the tall, burly man she addressed as Frederick meant little or nothing to her. In common with Romeo and his Juliet, he and Julia had locked glances for the first time and they had fallen in love forever! And what of Laura?

There were duties he owed his bride.

"No," he whispered. "Not yet, oh, God, not yet."

He suddenly thought of a solution. Given the fine weather they were enjoying, he would try to reach his home as soon as possible. Then he would give Laura some excuse regarding a need to visit some outlying properties on his estate. He would explain that his tenants were giving him trouble. In that way he could postpone the need of betraying Julia by making love to his wife.

A short time later Eric was bitterly reprimanding himself for decisions that bordered on madness. He had undertaken a responsibility and her name was Laura, and even if he did not love her, would never love her, he would try to be her husband—at least until there was an heir.

By the time they came in sight of the great stone posts with their wrought-iron, spear-tipped gates fronting the winding carriageway to Lord Marne's house, the present holder of the title was in a morose and self-accusatory mood.

Eric was, in fact, bitterly regretting what he now termed the aberration that seized him on what, for want of a better description, might be called his wedding night. Though his young bride, still sleeping in her virgin bed, had had no notion of his thoughts on that occasion, he was still only too aware of the injustice he had done her. He, who had courted her for no other reason than the fact that he needed an heir, had been prepared to be unfaithful to her and with her sister Julia!

A sigh escaped him. He had been quite sure that he would never fall in love again, and now, upon mature reflection, he told himself that he had *not* fallen in love with Julia, and indeed, he had no notion of ever seeking her out. It had been an attraction based mainly on her astonishing likeness to Christina and on her beguiling little ways, something of which she, in her innocence, was, he knew, completely unaware.

Furthermore, it was not of Julia he must think. He

must consider Laura, whom he had liked from the start. It was not her fault that try as he had for the past twenty-four hours, he could not obliterate the memory of his beloved Christina, a memory that was growing more vivid with every revolution of the carriage wheels! And here, where once it had seemed perfectly natural to bring his bride to his home, it now seemed completely unnatural and an insult to the memory of poor Christina. He had a fugitive wish to tell his driver to turn the carriage around and go as fast as was possible in some other direction!

Cornwall.

He actually shuddered as he wondered what had put that thought into his head. Cornwall and Julia, Julia-Christina. Think of neither, he ordered himself furiously.

"Oh!" Laura suddenly exclaimed excitedly as the gatekeeper, alerted by the coachman's horn, appeared to open the gates. "Oh," she repeated as the coach moved forward up a curving driveway, "such tall trees! These are the woods of which you spoke, Eric?"

"They are a small part of them," he said with a surge of pride and pleasure at seeing the gate house. Though he owned houses in London and in Yorkshire, here was his home, where he had grown up, and it was here that he had brought his dearest Christina! He avoided looking at Laura as, unwillingly, he envisioned Christina sitting beside him as she had been on that first day of their marriage. Resolutely he banished that all too persistent image and smiled at Laura as he continued. "There are other woods beyond the castle, which, as I have explained, is really a house, save for the keep, which lies in ruins a short distance from the newer buildings. Ah, and here's old Peebles, the gatekeeper, come back to greet us. You must give him a nod and a smile as lady of the house."

Laura smiled shyly as the carriage came to a stop. The gatekeeper's face was deeply lined and his hair was white. His eyes, deep blue, sparkled as he looked up at his master. "Ah, 'tis good to see ye, my lord."

"It's good to see you, Peebles, good to be home again," Eric said warmly. "This is Lady Marne, my wife."

"Ah, it's welcome ye are, milady." The gatekeeper smiled back at her.

"I thank you, Peebles. I am pleased to meet you," Laura told him shyly.

In another few moments they were passing more trees, elms and oaks and red beeches on either side of the carriageway. Then the road turned abruptly and Laura saw the house that had taken the place of the castle—a long, tall building, its facade blindingly reflecting the sun from two rows of windows above and below and causing galaxies of red and blue spots to dance before Laura's eyes. A small mansard roof with dormer windows was encased by a marble fence running the length of the house, and she counted six windows and almost as many chimneys. As he had explained, it was not a castle, but she did glimpse what appeared to be part of a keep on one side of the edifice, partially hidden by a pair of elms. And was she to live in this giant's dwelling? she wondered nervously. It did appear so very big—much larger than her home in the country. Inadvertently she shivered.

"Why are you shivering on such a warm day, my dear Laura?" Eric asked.

"Someone walked over my grave." She shrugged and subsequently was amazed and chagrined to see anger flash in Eric's eyes.

"That is an old wives' tale!" he exclaimed. "Death has no place in this homecoming, my dear Laura."

She swallowed an obstruction in her throat. Eric had seemed so angry, and it was not the first time she had aroused his ire with some foolish remark. "I meant nothing by it," she said apologetically.

"No, no, of course you did not, my dear," he apologized hastily, slipping his arm around her waist. "You must forgive me. I am never at my best on long journeys. We will both need to rest once we are indoors. Would you not like that, my dear?"

"Oh, yes, it would be pleasant," she agreed shyly.

"I think I have not told you about the servants, or have I?"

"No, you have not," she said.

"Well, they are under the rule of Mrs. Wilson, who has been in the household since my father's time. She is a most capable woman. Of course, you might want to make some changes in the staff. It is your prerogative, of course."

"Oh, no, I am sure I will find all your arrangements most satisfactory," she said quickly, feeling and not knowing quite why he did not want any changes in the staff.

"Very good," he said approvingly. "My wife . . . my late wife was of your mind. She did not trouble herself over household arrangements. She was content to leave everything to Mrs. Wilson."

"Did you live here most of the year?" Laura asked.

"Yes, Christina was extremely fond of the country, as I hope you will be too."

"Oh, yes, I much prefer it to London," she could tell him with perfect truth.

"Indeed?" He regarded her quizzically, almost as if, she thought, he did not quite believe her. "Do you really?"

"I really do. As you know, I do enjoy riding." She flushed, reminded of her fall in the park, the fall that had somehow resulted in his offer. She continued, "I am not generally as clumsy as I was in the park that day, and I do prefer a less restricted area. I shall enjoy riding through these woods."

"I hope you will also enjoy inviting some of the families who live nearby. In my wife . . . in Christina's day we rather neglected our social obligations. We were both so young and . . ."

"You wanted to be together," Laura finished, feeling a slight twinge of regret that he obviously did not regard her in that same light—but of course she was being foolish. As her mother had told her more than once, he was not marrying for love. He needed an heir.

"Ah," Eric said. "Here we are."

Laura gazed out of the window and found herself a few paces away from a huge oaken door and realized that they were directly in front of the great house that she was now to call home. As the carriage drew to a stop, Bob, one of the footmen, opened the door and set the steps before it. Eric, climbing out, helped Laura down the steps at the same time that the front door swung open, and in the aperture stood a tall, dignified man of about sixty-four or sixty-five, Laura thought. He was beaming at Eric.

"Your lordship and milady, welcome home!" he exclaimed warmly.

Eric smiled back at him. "Thank you, Wilson." He turned to Laura. "My dear, this is Mr. Wilson, our butler. He has been here since . . . before I was born."

Laura smiled up at him. "I am glad to meet you, Wilson."

"It is my pleasure, your ladyship." The butler bowed and added, "The others will be in the hall, sir."

"Yes, of course." Eric nodded. He added, "You will need to stand back, Wilson, as I carry my bride inside."

"Oh, must you?" Laura asked worriedly, all too aware of her weight, which she feared might even have increased during their two and a half days on the road. The meals she had eaten had been delicious, and she had not stinted herself.

"I must, my dear. It is a custom."

"Well, if you must . . ." she began, and then gasped as Eric easily lifted her and carried her over the threshold, setting her down just inside a vast hall with patterned marble floors and a wide staircase winding gracefully up to the first floor.

However, much as Laura wanted to look longer at a sculptured plaster ceiling and its huge center chandelier, she could not ignore the servants, a large group of men and women, some elderly and a great many quite young —footmen, housemaids, under-housemaids, a heavyset

woman who looked like a cook and standing with three
grinning young underlings who must be her helpers. And,
of course, the woman coming forward, small and probably in her late fifties, with a plain pleasant face and a
welcoming smile, must be the housekeeper. Her black
gown and her white apron and the keys at her waist
proclaimed her position.

"Your ladyship." She curtsied.

Eric said, "Here is Mrs. Wilson, our housekeeper, my
dear."

"Mrs. Wilson," Laura repeated. "I am glad to know
you . . . would you be related to the butler?"

"I am that, your ladyship. We have been wed these
forty years come September. And it's glad I am to
welcome you. As you can see, our staff bids you welcome
too."

In the next half hour Laura, repeating names and
greeting each member of the household, promised herself to procure a list of each name and position, something her mother had suggested she do. It had been an
ordeal she had feared, but it had passed quickly enough,
and the group disbanded with only Mr. and Mrs. Wilson
remaining. She had read approval in the housekeeper's
eyes, and she was much relieved, for she had feared she
would be compared most unfavorably to the beautiful
Christina.

"I have a small repast prepared, my lord," the housekeeper said. "If you would care to partake of it now, it is
ready."

"That would be delightful, Mrs. Wilson," Eric replied,
"but I think it were best if we rested for an hour or two. It
has been a long and tiring journey." He turned to Laura.
"Unless you would care for something now, my dear?"

"Oh, no," she assured him hastily. "I feel much in
need of a rest, myself." She glanced at Lucy, standing
near the door, and added regretfully, "Oh, dear, I fear I
have been remiss. Lucy!" she called. As the girl came to
her side she added, "This is Lucy Browne, my abigail,
Mrs. Wilson."

"Good afternoon, my dear," the housekeeper said cordially as Lucy bobbed a curtsy. "Should you like to come with me, then?"

"Oh, no, ma'am," Lucy said shyly. "I'd best do for 'er ladyship."

"Very well." Mrs. Wilson gave her an approving smile. "If you wish to find me later, one of the footmen will direct you."

"I do thank you, ma'am." Lucy curtsied.

"Come, then, my dear." Eric took Laura's arm, and followed by his valet and by Lucy, they walked up the wide stairs to the first floor. On reaching the top, he dismissed his valet, telling him to show Lucy to her ladyship's chamber. "I thought," he said as he turned back to Laura, "you might want to see some part of the house—your house, my dear."

She was very tired, but instinctively she felt that he was proud of his home and eager to note her reaction.

"I most certainly do want to see it," she assured him.

Some forty minutes later Laura stood alone in a large bedchamber, beyond which lay a sitting room, and beyond that, her husband's suite of rooms. She had not seen these, but he had shown her a great deal of the first floor, taking her through the drawing room, which, in common with that of her own house, opened onto a small antechamber and thence into the dining room. She was pleased by the arrangement mainly because she was used to it. The chambers in the newer houses did not lead one into the next but were set off from each other with doors opening on long halls. On the same line with the dining room was the conservatory, which Eric had showed her with some little reluctance.

"This was one of my wife's favorite chambers." He had indicated the numerous plants standing in pots on long tables, or hung in the windows, or rising from the floor. Little cards attached to each bush or flower indicated their Latin designation, their common name, and the family to which they belonged. These, written in a flowing hand, were, Eric explained, the work of the late Lady Marne. He had added, "She bought many of these, and the others were from her conservatory at home. She called this her winter garden, and she took wonderful care of her plants. *They* are still healthy and flourishing." His suggestion that he wished his wife might have remained in a similar condition had made Laura extremely uncomfortable. Indeed, she had longed to cut short the tour until he was better rested, but she was wary about putting herself forward. He might resent such suggestions from her. In fact, as she left the conservatory, she had a most uncomfortable suspicion that Eric, in his own mind, still regarded himself as the husband of the late Christina. She did come to the conclusion that she would not tend the plants in the conservatory. She would leave that to the servants, mainly because she was sure he would not want her to undertake that particular task.

He had managed to subdue his woe when he showed her the library, which lay just beyond the portrait gallery. He had taken her through the gallery with a swiftness she regretted, but she had momentarily forgotten her wish to see the portrait of his late wife, as she found herself among masses of books—books she had itched to examine, but again the progress through the library had been similarly swift. She had seen the large desk, with drawers that must contain writing paper. There had been a silver inkstand on top of the desk, and she had glimpsed several feathered pens. Her mother would be expecting a letter from her, and so would her grandmother, and though she had refuted the idea of being a bluestocking, she would not mind trying to write.

She sighed. She wished she had not thought of bluestockings, for that brought Julia to mind. Julia, who had been angry on her wedding day, who had refused to catch her bouquet, and who had looked at her as if she hated her, but, Laura reminded herself, she would be hating her at a distance—since Cornwall lay at least as far from Somerset as London. Yet on thinking of it, she realized that Julia was no more than two days away. If she should take it into her mind . . . but of course she would not want to visit *her*, and it was ridiculous to borrow trouble. She had trouble enough already with a husband who did not love her, could never love her, since there appeared to be room in his heart only for his Christina.

Furthermore, she must not resent Christina even if her hold on him was the stronger because of her early and tragic death. As she must needs remind herself, with the exception of a very few in her circles, love meant very little. Men married for the dowry and the heritage, and she had both. She also had a husband who was her friend. Given her appearance, she could ask for nothing more. Hard on that thought, she remembered Mrs. Wilson's mention of a repast. She had not been hungry then, but she was finding herself quite hungry now.

Had she better ask Eric if he wished to have something to eat, or would it be better . . . a tap on the door, the door which led to the sitting room, scattered her thoughts. She opened it hastily and found Eric there. He was looking regretful. "My dear," he said, "the most unfortunate set of circumstances has arisen."

A pulse in her throat began to pound. "What has happened?" she asked in some alarm.

"Ah, you must not worry," he said hastily. "A matter of great importance has come up, and I must leave first thing in the morning, which means that I will have to retire early. The exigencies of travel make it imperative that I have all the rest I can get. I fear I will have to remain by myself this night." He cleared his throat nervously. "I . . . I hope you will not mind."

Laura, looking up at him, found his glance evasive. She said, "I quite understand. I, myself, am very tired. I do hope you sleep well. Will you be gone long?"

"No, I should be back by tomorrow evening at the latest." He moved to her and bore her hand to his lips. "I do thank you for your understanding, my dear—and now, would you like to come downstairs for a little supper?"

"Oh, yes, very much," Laura assured him brightly.

Later, upon retiring, Laura evaded Lucy's surprised gaze and talked brightly of all she had seen in the house, adding that she hoped to visit the gardens and the woods on the following day. "And when I am a little more rested, I think I will go riding."

"It looks to be a fine place for riding, milady," Lucy commented.

Laura nodded. "Oh, yes, indeed it does." She had caught a strain of sympathy in the abigail's tone that she wished were not present. *She* did not feel sorry for herself. The fact that she had not experienced a wedding night in every sense of the word was hardly a tragedy. It was obvious that Eric was too disturbed by all the reminders of his lost wife to make love to her replacement—if one could call her that. One had to be in love to make love, and while she was sure Eric liked her, she was equally sure that he did not love her. But they were friends, and that was something.

In many marriages contracted by those of her class, the participants were actually enemies. Eric was certainly not her enemy. He only missed his first wife, whom he so rarely mentioned but whose presence had been with them throughout every minute of their journey from London and was even stronger here. *Christina.*

Laura had never believed in ghosts—despite the fact that many of her friends and acquaintances mentioned "drafts" in windowless rooms and mysterious "cold spots" which they believed signified the lingering presence of some family skeleton turned spirit.

Her house in the country had remained singularly free of such entities, but she did believe in pervasive memories, which could, on occasion, be more powerful than ghosts. Her mother was afflicted by memories of her late husband, and though she never mentioned these to her daughters, Laura had always been able to tell when Lady Roswell had dreamed of him—by her mood on the following day.

Christina was just such a memory, she was sure; and sure, too, that the objects she had touched, the corridors through which she had walked and the conservatory where she had tended her plants, each so painstakingly identified, was replete with her presence. Tears of sympa-

thy stood in her eyes, and she blinked them away hastily
for fear Lucy might believe she was weeping for herself.

On rising at eight the following morning, Laura
learned that Eric had left the house at six. She found
herself in an odd mood—caught somewhere between
disappointment and relief. His sorrow for his wife had
filled her with sympathy, but at the same time, it was
difficult to offer consolation for a loss that had provided
her with a husband she loved, even though he would
never feel the same about her. Still, he had rescued her
from a fate she had anticipated from her fifteenth year
onward. She had believed herself doomed to follow in
the wake of other plain girls whose purpose in life was to
be a "prop" to Mama.

Lady Nell Colgrave, one of her good friends, occupied
such an unenviable position. Her mother, a confirmed
invalid who lay all day on a couch of pain, had need of
such a prop. Lady Roswell, on the other hand, did not.
Her busy, bustling parent had heaved many a sigh when
she believed Laura not attending. It had been obvious
that she had had little belief in her daughter's ability to
get a husband, and Jane's prediction had angered her—
because of what she had imagined to be the futility of
introducing her plain daughter to the London scene for
the whole of an unfruitful season. Now she was preening
herself like a peacock because, of her three daughters,
Laura had made the most brilliant match!

"Married for an heir, married for an heir, married for
an heir." The words beat against Laura's consciousness,
but though tears threatened, she would not let them fall!
She had very little to weep about. She was in a lovely
house, which she had not seen in its entirety, and which
she would explore in her leisure, of which she had plenty.
She would start now—or as soon as she was dressed—
and she would begin with the portrait gallery. Above
everything in this household, she wanted most to view
the portrait of the late Lady Marne. She rang for Lucy.

Fortunately the portraits were grouped by centuries,
and though a quick glance promised future rewards,

Laura passed hastily along the polished floor of the long chamber until she found the painting she sought. It proved very easy to locate—mainly because the late Christina had chosen to be painted as a nymph, posed amid trees and holding a book in her hand, which she was not perusing. Yet she gave the impression of having been interrupted while reading just for the second (minutes, hours, days) it took for the artist to capture her on canvas. Her hair, long and golden, was caught by a vagrant breeze, and one yellow lock strayed across her forehead. Her great eyes were vividly blue, and a small, mysterious smile played about her lips. She seemed caught in some happy dream, and she did remind Laura of a nymph—more specifically, she reminded her of Julia! And was that why when her sister had appeared at the wedding reception, Eric had become so thoughtful and distracted, a condition that yet remained? Tears filled her eyes. She had been right to fear Julia!

Yet on second thought, Julia was married, and she could not leave her house at a moment's notice to visit her sister, or how would she explain it to Frederick? She gazed up at the portrait, and those great eyes, Julia's eyes, seemed to be telling her that she had always done exactly as she pleased and in that way she, Christina, was no different from Julia.

She left the gallery, moving swiftly, almost on a run, and went into the library. However, for once in her life the wealth of reading matter, which, in other circumstances, must have absorbed her completely, did not interest her. She left the library and was met by a harried-looking young footman, who appeared very pleased to see her.

"If you please, your ladyship, there'll be a visitor. Lady Orville come to see you."

"To see *me?*" Laura demanded in some surprise. It was no more than half past the hour of ten, and certainly she had not anticipated visitors on this, her first day in her husband's home! Yet she must needs get to know her neighbors. Perhaps Lady Orville had been Christina's

good friend and might inadvertently let fall some information about her.

"I will see her . . . George, is it?"

"Aye, your ladyship." He looked gratified by her
accurate recollection of his name. "George it be, right
enough. I'll show her into the drawing room, shall I?"

"Please, and tell her that I will be there directly."

Returning to her chamber, Laura scanned herself in
the glass and pushed back a fallen lock of hair with a sigh.
She feared that Lady Orville would find her a poor
replacement for the beauty. Sighing a second time, she
went down to meet her first guest.

As Laura started into the drawing room she thought as
she had yesterday afternoon that it badly needed refur-
bishing. It was decorated in gold and white—not
Christina's taste, Eric had told her. She had not cared to
change the furnishings, though. She had been content to
let his late mother's taste prevail. Laura thought some of
the chairs needed recovering, and a repainting would
certainly enhance the dingy woodwork. Yet she wondered if her husband wanted such repairs. She had a
feeling that he might prefer everything to remain as it
had during Christina's lifetime, and once more she
wondered nervously what Lady Orville would think
about her. Probably she had been a dear friend of the late
Lady Marne and was here as a scout to spread the news
about the present wife. Looking around, she did not see
her visitor.

Then, suddenly, and with the swiftness of a nesting
quail disturbed by a hunter's gun, a tall woman who had
been sitting in a wing chair rose and said in a deep voice,
"You are Lady Marne?"

Laura, tensing and barely swallowing an incipient cry
of surprise as she looked up at a tall, attractive young
woman who she guessed to be no more than twenty-four
or five, said, "Yes, I am Lady Marne."

"Well!" Lady Orville said, "I am extremely pleased to
see you. It is time that the mournful Marne doffed his
weeds and loosed his turtledoves. Did I startle you? I am

sorry, it was not intentional. On occasion it *is* intentional. From my early youth there has been nothing more exhilarating to me than to create an unforgettable impression. I should have been an actress, but birth and breeding prevented my being a 'poor player that struts and frets his hour upon the stage and then is heard no more . . . a tale told by an idiot' and so forth. I fear you will imagine that I am that idiot. Have I?"

"I . . . I am not sure." Laura found herself swallowing a threatening giggle. "I am not sure what you mean."

"Then I have not created an unforgettable impression?"

"Oh, you have." Laura's giggle escaped.

"Ah, very good! Do you know that I once tried this same entrance—I am known for my entrances—on the late Lady Marne, and to my utter chagrin, I do not believe she noticed. But enough, I am extremely pleased to meet you. I know that I have already said as much, but this time I mean it in all sincerity."

"I am also pleased to meet you." Laura was surprised, amused, and, she decided, extremely drawn to her ladyship, despite her eccentric manner.

"I would think you were less pleased than surprised," Lady Orville said frankly. "You have not been here more than a day. You arrived yesterday, and lest you be astonished that news travels so fast, let it be said that one of your footmen is walking out with my abigail, Betsy. That is the way news travels here. Betsy is a fund of useful information. You would be surprised to know what I know, and I would, no doubt, be surprised to know what is known about me. If you are minded to engage in a flirtation, be assured that I will hear about it directly the moment the first assignation is arranged—or almost. I and every other household from here to Glastonbury."

"I would not be so minded," Laura said.

"Not now, of course, when you are but recently married, but occasionally husbands can wear on one. I am not speaking of my own husband, Bruce, but in

general. You look as if you might possess a sense of
humor. Do you?"

"I expect I do." Laura smiled. "Will you not sit down,
Lady Orville?"

"Yes, I will." She sank back in the wing chair again.
"You will find that I have taken the most comfortable
chair in this chamber—however, that sofa is well enough
and we can face each other. I hope that you mean to
make some changes here. Christina was occupied with
higher things—comfort was not one of them. I am
pleased, too, that you are reasonably tall. The late
Christina was a little thing, you know."

"She did not look little in her portrait," Laura said
with some surprise.

"Oh, blast John Kildare. In common with Romney,
whose disciple he is, he is inclined to flatter his subjects.
No one will ever tell me that Lady Hamilton was ever as
exquisite as he depicted her. She was really quite common, and looked it. That is not to say that I approve the
shocking way in which she died in Calais last year. The
government ought to have honored Nelson's last wishes
—even if she were a whore, which she might have been in
one sense but not in another—and the nation has
honored whores before. I speak of Charles II, who was
always enobling his mistresses and their bastards. However, I expect it does take a king to do that, and George
III, poor man, is mad, and the prince is bad . . . not bad,
really. I expect that Nelson's wishes were not in his
power to grant. However, to comment upon your observation, Christina was quite small, and I do wish that
Kildare had not painted her in green. She wore it
incessantly afterward. I do hope that green is not one of
your favorite shades."

"Actually, it is not," Laura said, striving to swallow
her laughter.

"No, you would look far better in blue."

Fearing that the topic of Christina might soon be
exhausted due to Lady Orville's habit of leaping from
one subject to the next, Laura said hastily, "I expect you

must have known Christina rather well."

"No one knew Christina rather well," Lady Orville said. "In common with the poet Wordsworth, she was enchanted with nature and kept to herself a great deal, communing with the woods. I saw her only when I gave a dinner party. . . . She, I might mention, rarely entertained. She preferred to go to bed early so that she might be up at dawn; wandering through the 'dew-touched grasses'—her description, never mine. The only time I see the 'dew-touched grasses' is when I am off on a fox hunt. Oh, dear, you should not have asked me about Christina. I am inclined to become entirely too verbose on the subject." She paused and directed a piercing look at Laura. "I like you a great deal better."

"You do not know me!" Laura exclaimed.

"To see you is to like you," Lady Orville responded frankly. "I am extremely intuitive. And I am quite sure that marrying you is the most sensible thing that young Eric ever did—where is he, by the way?"

"He had to leave early this morning," Laura explained. "I . . . I think he must still miss her, you know." She flushed, wondering why she had favored Lady Orville with such a confidence. Had her mother heard her, she must have been shocked to the bone. "I mean—"

"My dear child," Lady Orville interrupted, "I am quite sure you meant exactly what you said, and unfortunately you are probably quite right. He took her death very hard, and of course it was tragic about the child—a son, I have heard. Still—and I am going to be quite unnaturally frank with you—he eventually would have suffered even more if she had lived. Men in love don blinders from time to time, but the day comes when those blinders fall off . . . Christina's early death precluded that. Consequently he never learned that rather than marrying a swan, he had wed a goose. Gracious me!" Lady Orville stood up. "We must be friends, else my husband, who is extremely fond of Eric, will never forgive me. You will not tell him what I have said out of my very real friendship for you . . . I do like you. You seem to grow more appealing by the minute—even though I have done all the talking. You must say that you will be my friend."

"But I am . . . I am already your friend," Laura cried. "I liked you the minute I saw you—and I like you even more now."

"I am delighted to hear it," Lady Orville returned with a lovely smile. "We live close to each other, close as it is read in the fewest miles distant. You can see the towers of our castle from the edge of your park. Of course, there is a great stretch of fields, pastures, et cetera, between. I am going to give one of my dinner parties and you will come and see the pile in which we reside. Unfortunately it was not destroyed in the days of Cromwell . . . though the Roundheads did practice shooting in the main hall. You will find bullet marks in the ancient suits of armor . . . where naught but spears had grazed before. Does that not sound as if I were talking about cows instead of spears? No matter, my dear Lady Marne, but you will not be Lady Marne to me, nor I Lady Orville to you. I am Millicent, hardly suitable for me, and you are . . ."

"Laura." The owner of that name laughed.

"Laura." Lady Orville cocked her head and studied Laura's face. "Yes," she said finally. "I do believe Laura does suit you. Millicent, on the other hand, should belong to someone small and fly away, another Christina, perhaps, but we do not choose our names, do we? I must leave." She bent and kissed Laura on the cheek. "My dear child, take heart. He cannot fail to appreciate you once he realizes his good fortune. And remember, I am Millicent to you, Laura."

"I . . . I will remember, Millicent," Laura said gratefully.

She felt much happier after Lady Orville left. She had made a friend, and one who had given her hope that upon due reflection, her husband might begin to feel more comfortable with her, even if he never learned to love her.

FIVE

ERIC WALKED THROUGH THE WOODS, his woods, on the way
to the house. The sun was darkly orange against the
western horizon, and the clouds were edged with its
dimming brightness. The leaves of the trees made an
elliptical pattern against the golden sky.

If Christina had been with him, she would have
mentioned the leaves, the murmuring, wind-shaken
leaves. She might also have spoken of the drowsy chirp-
ing of the birds—except that they were not really
drowsy, for twilight had yet to descend. Christina had
loved the twilight. He remembered her walking beside
him and quoting Wordsworth and other nature-loving
poets. In this moment he was remembering a passage
from Dante. It seemed singularly descriptive of his own
mood, and he muttered it under his breath as he reluctantly headed toward a path that must bring him out of
the woods.

" 'In the middle of the journey of life I came to myself
within a dark wood where the straight way was lost . . .' "
However, Dante had found someone to lead him forth
from the darkness and to show him a glimpse of heaven
—Virgil. No such mythic guide awaited him. Instead he
would be coming home to another woman, not Chris-

tina, one he would find easily enough when he came into his house.

Eric groaned. At this moment he found himself hating and even loathing his aunt and his sister for urging him to marry again. No, they had *not* urged, they had insisted that he do so. He had done their bidding, had married, and had not even dreamed what it might mean for him to install his new young wife here in a place Christina had made her own!

"Christina," he murmured. "Oh, Christina, where have you gone?"

As usual, there was no answer. There had been a time when in the depth of his grief he had fallen on his knees and begged her to return. He had reminded the silence that he had friends who spoke of lingering ancestral ghosts. He had begged Christina to haunt him, haunt the room she loved—the conservatory. He had spent night after night in there—praying, beseeching her elusive spirit to manifest itself, crying out for a sign, a rustle of a curtain on a windless night, a coldness on the floor in the heat of summer, a whisper in his ear!

Alas, she had remained as elusive in death as she had been in life. Much as he had loved her, he had never really plumbed the depths of her soul. She had remained elusive and mysterious, infinitely tantalizing. Indeed, she was the very antithesis of Laura, plump, matter-of-fact Laura, blunt of speech and not an ounce of mystery in her entire being!

He already knew her through and through and was uncomfortably aware that she loved him. He would eventually have to go through the motions, if not the emotions, of love and pretend to a passion he would never feel. Of course, Laura, frank and forthright, would not understand that. She and subtlety were strangers, and of course, she was half a child.

A memory of Bartholomew Fair brought with it a host of images. Laura had been so excited as they had visited the various booths and tents. Her eyes had been bright as stars as she gazed at the puppets, the waxworks, the dancers, and the freaks. No, he thought, not the freaks. It had been Christina who had found them so amusing when they had visited their tents during a county fair outside of Taunton.

Laura had been distressed to think of them being on display and suffering such long hours in a hot and ill-smelling tent. She had been highly indignant at the rude remarks and loud laughter their conditions invited. She had hurried him through the tent, but she had insisted that they give more money than was asked so that the poor pig-faced woman might be rewarded for her anguish. He had not had the heart to tell her that those who exploited the creature would probably pocket the money without giving her so much as a groat. He had not wanted to disillusion her and spoil the day's pleasure.

Had it been a pleasant day? Tolerably, he decided. She had been so excited and pleased that he had been pleased, too, and had enjoyed himself more than he had anticipated. Yet if he had met her sister Julia before the wedding . . .

It would have made no difference, he reminded himself quickly. Julia was married too. She lived in Cornwall . . . he hoped that she would remain in Cornwall, and forbore to dwell on the reasons for that hope. Quickening his steps, he strode out of the woods and was soon on the way to the north porch. He had not sent word that he was returning, mainly because he feared that Laura might come running to meet him as Christina had—drifting out of the doorway, gliding across the porch, as graceful as she was exquisite—a nymph, an houri, a goddess!

If Laura were less large, he might compare her to a . . . but he did not want to think of comparisons. It was not really fair. Laura was Laura, unexciting, unmysterious, rich, well born, and undoubtedly would be a good mother to the children she would give him. As for love, he had known it once and reveled in its glory. Such ecstasy could not occur twice in a lifetime. He must settle for affection. He did like Laura. She was immensely likable, immensely placid too. He doubted that she had a temperamental bone in her whole body. And she did have a nice little sense of humor, something Christina had never possessed—at least not in abundance, but that had never really mattered. And contrary to what Celia said, she was not dense. Christina had been dreamy. . . . He groaned as his late wife once more replaced Laura in his thoughts, bringing grief and frustration with her.

"Not yet . . . not yet," a voice deep inside him cried. "Another day, make love to Laura, but, please, please, my dear, not this night." Was that a voice in his head, or had Christina finally come to him? It did not matter, he would obey the command.

"You are looking unhappy today, Laura," Lady Orville said. "Did not your lord come home yesterday, as promised? But I am sure he did. My girl told me so. Servants always know, as I think I have told you. I am convinced they keep their ears to the ground, as it is said red Indians do in the wilds of America."

Laura smiled. One had to smile at Lady Orville's teasing, no matter how one felt. "He did return," she acknowledged, "but he was in one of his melancholy moods, and I really did not even see him. He went directly to his chamber, and his valet informed me that he was wearied from the exigencies of travel. When I rose this morning, I was told that he was conferring with his bailiff about some matters pertaining to the estate."

"Damn and blast the estate . . . damn and blast the exigencies of travel!" Lady Orville cried. "Of all the self-indulgent, totally selfish men who ever existed on this planet since the beginning of time, your so-called husband wins the golden apple! And I even hesitate to call him 'your husband'! He has yet to assume that mantle! If I were you, my dear, I would leave him to wallow in his grief . . ." She paused, looking into Laura's unhappy face. "Unfortunately I am not you, and I doubt that you will ever mete out to Eric the treatment he so richly deserves. I am going to give my threatened dinner, and I will subsequently present him with a piece of my mind which he might not find totally indigestible."

"Oh, I beg you will not," Laura protested.

"You may beg all you choose, my dear, but I will not heed you." Lady Orville glared at her. "You really do annoy me, Laura, much as I like you. If you had any backbone at all, you would. . . ." She sighed. "But never mind, let us enjoy the day and the ride." She paused and then added thoughtfully, "You could not possibly fall off your horse and come back muddied and with a few interesting bruises? That might gain his pity, but no, you are too damned straightforward to result to the underhanded. Still, 'hold! He that is coming must be provided for and you shall put this night's great business into my despatch,' which should have an excellent bearing on 'all your nights and days to come.' There are times, my dearest Laura, when it is better to be Lady Macbeth than Juliet."

Laura laughed and then sighed. "I have a sister, Julia. If only I resembled her. She has rather the look of his late wife."

"Then I will detest her sight unseen," Lady Orville said firmly. "Where does the creature live?"

"She lives in Cornwall."

"I hope she was not present at your wedding."

"I had hoped she would not come, myself, but—" Laura broke off. "I mean—"

"I am sure that you mean exactly what you say," Lady Orville interrupted. She continued. "I hope she lives on one of the Isles of Scilly."

"She does live in Land's End." Laura smiled.

"Well, that is almost as good. It is a reasonable distance from here, but not as far as Scotland. What a pity that she does not reside in the Highlands."

"You do not know Julia," Laura said, feeling a belated need to defend her if only on the grounds that she *was* her sister.

"Actually I feel that I do" was the enigmatic response. "Do you know, Laura, dear, since a suit of armor is used these days only for decorative purposes, it might be well

were you to develop some manner of interior armor. But
come, we have talked long enough. Let us be on our way.
Has your husband ever ridden with you?"

"In the park," Laura said, preferring not to describe
the ramifications attendant on that ride.

"He ought to ride with you here. You are a veritable
Amazon—but enough, I have had my say. Let us go."

"Please," Laura said. She had been finding Lady
Orville's barbed comments more disturbing than usual,
emphasizing as they did Eric's determined withdrawal
from her. It *was* time that he recognized the fact that
Christina was no more, and he was wed to another!

"Very good," Lady Orville commented.

"I beg your pardon?" Laura asked confusedly.

"My dear Laura, you have a face that speaks volumes.
I beg you will put your thoughts into words. I challenge
you, do it once we have returned from our ride."

"I will," Laura said, surprising herself.

"Lovely." Lady Orville's smile had become a grin.

Two hours later Laura, returning to the stables, felt
exhilarated by her ride and, furthermore, determined to
accede to her friend's persuasions and also to herself on
the subject of Eric's prolonged mourning. She was not
sure how best to approach the matter, but approach it
she would. As she rode into the stable yard, some of her
determination fled, for he was there, talking with one of
the grooms. A greeting trembled on her lips and was
swallowed as he turned quickly.

"Good morning, my dear." He came toward her, and
much to her relief, he was smiling.

"Good morning, Eric," she returned shyly, adding
unnecessarily, "I have been riding."

"So I see . . . and as usual your seat on a horse is
excellent. But why did you not take a groom with you?"

"I met Millicent . . . Lady Orville."

"Ah, Lady Orville. A pleasant young woman, I believe."

"She is extremely pleasant."

"Here. Let me help you down from your horse."

"That is not necessary, Eric," Laura said quickly, and hurriedly dismounted. The excitement of having her husband help her would be, alas, vitiated by the fact that he might need to hold her briefly. Her weight would be a sad strain on him, and he would certainly find the contrast between herself and the willowy Christina even more pronounced.

He laughed as she stood before him on the ground. "It seems that I have wed an independent woman." Moving forward, he took the reins from her hands and signaled to a groom. As the man led the horse away, he said, "You are already on a first-name basis with Lady Orville?"

"She insisted that we must be. I do find her charming." Laura spoke a little anxiously, realizing that she had not really known the lady long enough to use her given name.

"Well, that is as it should be. I do want you to become acquainted with the other families around here, my dear."

"Lady Orville has spoken of inviting us to dinner."

"Has she, indeed? Well, I am pleased. And you do like her?"

There was a thread of surprise winding through his words, and Laura, remembering that the late Christina had not warmed to the lady, said quickly. "Oh, yes, I do very much. She called here the first day, and I liked her immediately."

"Indeed?" He regarded her quizzically. "Well, I am pleased to hear it. Bruce, her husband, has long been my good friend—even though we have seen relatively little of each other in the last years. But do you not find Lady Orville singularly outspoken?"

From his tone Laura gathered that the late Christina had not been sparing in her comments. She hoped that he had not become totally prejudiced against her new friend. She said warmly, "Oh, no. I admire frankness."

"Do you? Well, then, I am sure that you and Lady Orville will become fast friends. I have been told that she is nothing if not frank."

"That is true." Laura laughed. "I find it very refresh-

ing. So many people think it necessary to say what they
believe a person would like to hear rather than what they
really think. Lady Orville does not scruple to tell the
truth. And I have always preferred honesty to facile
compliments."

"I must agree," he said. He added abruptly, "I hope
you are not weary from your ride?"

"Oh, not at all! I do love to ride, and your horses are so
easy to control."

"I imagine rather that *you* find them easy to control.
But, my dear, what would you say to a drive around the
district? I would like to show you some of the sights of
which we who are Somerset-born are very proud."

"Oh"—Laura smiled.—"I should like that above all
things."

"Above *all* things?" Eric repeated with a smile. "You
are remarkably easy to please, my dear Laura."

Laura wished that she dared tell him that her pleasure
in the forthcoming excursion came from the promise of
his company, but shyness put its usual harness on her
tongue. She said diffidently, "I have always wanted to
know more about Somerset."

"I hope I will have increased your knowledge by the
time the day is over," he said genially.

It was delightful to sit with Eric in the post chaise.
Laura had expected he would ride outside as he had done
throughout much of their journey from London. However, there was no saddle horse attached to the vehicle, and
Eric, pointing out various points of interest to her,
seemed perfectly content to be at her side. Indeed, she
was reminded of the time when he had taken her up in
his curricle and driven her around London. She had little
dreamed that the invitation was tantamount to a propo-
sal of marriage. He had been very companionable that
day, and he seemed in that same mood now as they came
into Glastonbury.

"We will stop here," he said, breaking into Laura's
thoughts. As the coachman dutifully brought the vehicle
to a halt, Eric opened the door and sprang out, saying as

the startled footman put the steps up, "I will help my wife to descend."

Laura, flushed with excitement, put out her hand and felt her flush deepen as her husband seized it in his warm grasp. She was further thrilled when, after instructing the coachman where and when to await him, he took her arm, saying, "I do hope you will enjoy this little excursion. My father took me to Glastonbury when I was eleven or thereabouts, and I can still remember how excited I was to be in a place where King Arthur and Queen Guinevere were supposed to have been buried. I had yet to learn that they had no more reality than Jack the Giant Killer."

"We cannot be sure about that," Laura said shyly.

His smile was gently derisive. "Oh, and will you tell me that you belong to those who believe that if England's soldiers are ever driven to the wall by an alien invader, King Arthur and his knights will rise from sleep and go galloping to her rescue?"

"I do not believe that, but still, someone similar to King Arthur might have lived," Laura said. "It was all such a very long time ago."

"I am not saying that I would not *like* to believe in them," Eric said thoughtfully.

"They do say that there is always a grain of truth to every legend," Laura commented.

"A rather small grain, I would think. "But come, let us walk."

"Please," Laura said with alacrity.

It was a pretty place, and it drew a great many sightseers on this warm day. Several young women had set up easels and were doing watercolors of the Abbey ruins, something Laura wished she might do. Julia was adept at painting and had already produced some excellent watercolors. Several of these hung in the parlor at home, and a visiting artist had commented upon her ability. Laura wished she had not thought of Julia. Every time she did, her old feelings of inadequacy swept over her.

"My dear"—Eric's voice scattered these unhappy thoughts—"there on that high hill is where the Abbot died."

"The Abbot?" she questioned.

"Yes. I expect you know that Glastonbury was one of the most celebrated ecclesiastical centers in Europe—some three to four hundred years ago."

"Yes, I have read about it and how Joseph of Arimathea brought the thorns from the crown of the Savior and planted the thorn tree."

"He also brought the spear which Lungius thrust into Jesus' side—according to the legends." He shook his head. "You would not think that a shrine so famous and an abbey so rich could have been leveled to the ground because Henry VIII chose to divorce Catherine of Aragon."

"And all because she could not give him a son," Laura murmured.

"I think it was less that and more Anne Boleyn." He smiled. "But come . . . there"—he pointed to the hill—"facing us is the place where the last Abbot of Glastonbury Abbey was hanged. Do you know that if you talk to one or another of the folk who live here, they will speak of his execution as if it happened the day before yesterday?"

"It must have been a great shock to them, especially as many of them could not have approved of it." Laura shuddered.

Eric, glancing at her, suddenly put his fingers under her chin, tilting her face toward him. "Do I see tears?" he asked.

Laura blushed. "Well, it . . . it does seem so sad to think of that rich, powerful man being drawn up the hill on a hurdle and hanged in full view of the town."

"Ah, you, too, are familiar with the story, I see."

She nodded. "Yes, I have always enjoyed reading history, and I am partial to the early Tudor and Elizabethan periods."

"Indeed, I find that era particularly interesting, myself. Though I must admit that my admiration was mainly fixed on the daring exploits of Sir Francis Drake. I might mention that you will find many histories in our library —some are very old. My grandfather was a well-known collector of ancient manuscripts."

"Oh, really?" Laura said excitedly. "I will look forward to reading them."

"If you can find them." He frowned slightly. "I have always meant to have the library catalogued, but I fear I have neglected it. Christina was not much of a reader, save for her books on plants, but I can remember my father reading to us. He had a fine voice. My sister and I used to be enthralled by the way he made history come alive."

"Oh, that must have been enjoyable. I think my father was also interested in history. At least that is what Mama has told me. She also says that I take after him—with my nose always in a book."

"You never knew your father?"

"No, he succumbed to a virulent fever a month before I was born."

"Oh, that is a pity."

"It was worse for my sisters. Julia, especially. She was his favorite."

"She remembers him?"

"Actually she remembers him quite well, even though she had just turned six when he died," Laura explained, wishing devoutly that she had not introduced the dangerous topic of Julia. Eric was looking extremely interested, and she could not help recalling that moment at the wedding when Julia had dropped the bouquet. She shivered.

"Are you cold, my dear? The wind is a little cool," Eric said solicitously.

"No, not in the least," Laura hastened to assure him, glad that the dangerous topic of Julia had been abandoned.

They left the scene of the Abbot's misfortune and wandered to the so-called sacred spring, where miracles of healing were purported to have occurred, and finally they had supper at an old inn called the George and

Pilgrim where, said the host, the ghost of a monk occasionally startled travelers there for the night.

They laughed together over that, and then Laura said, "I do not believe in ghosts, do you?" She was distressed to see his face change and his eyes grow somber. He said slowly, "No, I cannot think there are ghosts—at least I have never encountered one." Meeting her eyes, he continued in a rather bitter tone of voice, "That should please you, my dear. Your home is free from visitants, specters, and the like . . . the dead sleep peacefully and the living . . . mourn."

Laura tensed. It would have taken someone far less sensitive than herself not to realize that inadvertently she had opened an old wound. No, it was not so old. His beloved Christina had been gone less than three years, and when, she wondered unhappily, would she ever learn tact? Then, and with a trace of indignation, she decided that her remark had not been untactful; it merely had been something anyone would say!

"I am in total agreement," Lady Orville said the following day after listening to Laura's tearful account of Eric's moody silence on the way home. "I am going to do as I earlier threatened, my poor child. I am going to give a dinner party. Eric has not been near us for quite a while, and as he told you, he has been a good friend of Bruce—but dear Christina's pronounced dislike of me has kept him away." She bent an eye on Laura. "It has not been a week, and yet I see a diminution of your weight. I hope you have not been starving yourself?"

"I have not been very hungry, that is all," Laura explained.

"Well, the loss is not unbecoming," Lady Orville observed. "I hope, however, that you will not try to be a sylph."

"I doubt that I could." Laura laughed.

"Ah, I am pleased to have made you laugh. Your husband is going to have a piece of my mind, I assure you."

"Please, no," Laura protested. "It must be so difficult

for him—seeing someone else in Christina's place."

"And"—Lady Orville frowned—"it must be so easy for you having to be subjected to his fits and starts."

Laura looked down. "I do not mind. I want him to be happy."

"And if this prolonged grieving makes him happy, you will stand meekly by and . . . oh, dear, what is the use? Neither of you has any connection with reason, but I will put a flea in the ear of my husband, as the saying goes. It is possible that Bruce might succeed where others have failed!"

Since it would have proved futile to argue with Lady Orville, Laura did not make the effort, but as she returned to the stable, she still held the unhappy conviction that despite his determined efforts—and on occasion they had been determined—Eric would never be comforted for the loss of his wife. She had captured both his imagination and his heart, and by dying so early and so tragically, she would retain them forever!

On dismounting from her horse, she noticed a pony cart in the stable yard. It was drawn by a milk-white pony with a silky mane. The cart was painted a dark green and gave the impression of being new—from its padded leather seat to the collar, bridle, and reins.

"Do we have a guest, then?" Laura asked Jim, one of the stable lads.

He shook his head. "'E be 'ere for the books, 'e said."

"The books?" Laura questioned, but ceased her interrogation as she saw a blank look in Jim's eyes.

"The books?" Laura murmured to herself as she entered the house through a side door, wishing as always that she might have some of the shabby furniture taken out and the curtains changed. There was a preponderance of green in the house, which, she reminded herself, was less Christina's doing than Eric's mother's, but again she forbore to mention changes lest she win her husband's approval but at the same time increase his despondency. He would feel it was her right to request them, just as he would believe it his obligation to provide them. Meanwhile she would be, in effect, trespassing on the territory which Christina still claimed. She sighed. It would be easier to say nothing and put up with the green.

As she came into the main hall Laura met a footman and remembered the pony cart. "Jim told me that we have a visitor, George. Who might he be?"

"'E's come to catalogue the library, milady," he explained.

"Oh, really," Laura said excitedly, and hurried up the stairs and into that vast chamber, pausing on the threshold as she saw Eric speaking with a short young man dressed in the height of fashion. However, as she drew nearer, she realized that despite his natty appearance, his garments bore signs of being mended and even patched at the knees. Still, he bore himself proudly, making the most of inches, which, she thought, did not much exceed five feet five. His hair was fashionably cut and a light auburn in hue, and the glance he turned on her was a dark hazel. On seeing her, he bowed and smiled.

Eric, too, smiled. "My dear, this is Mr. Thomas Quinn, who will be our new librarian."

"I will, your lordship?" Mr. Quinn asked in startled accents, and then blushed. "I beg your pardon, my lord, but I did not realize that you had reached a decision."

"Oh, but I have," Eric assured him. "You appear to be extremely knowledgeable, and since my wife and I are great readers, we are anxious to have the mysteries of this library probed. As I have already explained, it has been sadly neglected since my grandfather's day. When will you be able to begin on your labors?"

"Today," Mr. Quinn blurted, and then blushed again. "Tomorrow, my lord. I must see to lodgings."

"But you may stay here, of course," Eric said. "Is that not usual?"

"It is not entirely unusual, my lord, but I have done so only on a few occasions."

"We have a great many unoccupied chambers here, and there is no need to stay at an inn or in other accommodations unless you would prefer to do so."

"Oh, my lord, I would not!" Mr. Quinn said warmly. "I should enjoy being here. As an antiquarian, I am much enamored of the great mansions that one sees in various parts of the country, and this house is a particularly felicitous example of its kind."

"In the name of my ancestors, I thank you." Eric smiled. "But I give you leave to take your time in settling in. You need not commence your work immediately."

"Oh, but I should prefer to do so, my lord." Mr. Quinn looked around him. "There is so very much here to beguile and enchant a scholar such as myself."

"Is there not!" Laura exclaimed. "I anticipate that you will find some old books—very old, I mean. Perhaps there will be some incunabula."

"I should not be surprised, milady." Mr. Quinn gazed eagerly at the rather disordered shelves. "I anticipate a veritable trove of treasures."

"It might take you some time to discover them," Eric commented.

"That is part of the excitement." Mr. Quinn's eyes shone.

"I can see you will attack your work with enthusiasm." Eric smiled. "There is a chance that you will find a grimoire. I hope it will not frighten you."

"A grimoire?" Laura questioned. "There are books on witchcraft here?"

"Ah, you are acquainted with the subject?" Eric asked her.

"No, not precisely, but I have read about them in Gothic novels."

"Ah." Eric laughed. "But of course they would figure largely in those."

"How old is the grimoire?" Mr. Quinn asked interestedly.

"I am not sure. It was the property of my great-grandmother, and she, I might add, was not a witch. It seems she appropriated it from a maidservant during our annual celebration of St. John's Eve."

"Ah, you celebrate St. John's Eve here, then?" Mr. Quinn asked.

"Yes, every summer. It is a tradition at the castle. We still call ourselves a castle," Eric explained. "We set the bonfire in a clearing near the keep. . . ." He turned to Laura. "I do not believe I have told you about that, have I, my dear?"

"No," she said, "and St. John's Eve is no more than three weeks away."

"Yes, that is true. However, you'll not need to concern yourself with the preparations. The servants will attend to it. That, too, is a tradition."

"Will there be dancing around the bonfire?" Laura asked.

Eric frowned and then nodded. "Yes, there always is."

Laura concealed a sigh and wondered how many times she would unwittingly say something that must bring the late Christina forcibly to her husband's mind. She could imagine the graceful nymph of the portrait whirling around the bonfire. Unfortunately she could also see herself and hoped devoutly that she would be allowed to watch from the sidelines.

"I expect," Mr. Quinn said, breaking the small silence that had followed Eric's comment, "that I had best be going. I will have to settle with the innkeeper. Are you sure that it is convenient for me to come this afternoon, my lord?"

"I am quite sure, Mr. Quinn. We will have a room prepared for you."

Once Mr. Quinn, all smiles and words of gratitude, had gone, Eric turned to Laura. "Well, my dear, the library will soon be in order. The young man has excellent references, though I believe he is a little down on his luck."

"I had the same impression myself," Laura said. "I hope that you intend to pay him well."

"Of course."

"Oh, I am pleased." She gazed around the immense

room. The books were not only not in proper order—some of them were piled on the floor, something she had not wanted to bring to her husband's attention lest he believe that she was, in effect, criticizing the late Christina for her neglect of the volumes. She was rather sure that the conservatory had absorbed Christina's entire attention. Consequently the fact that Eric had hired a librarian was very cheering. She had been half afraid that he might want the house to remain a sort of shrine to his late wife.

"A penny for your thoughts, my dear," Eric said.

She looked up quickly. "They are not worth half the sum," she murmured, and was glad that he could not read them.

"I would dispute that." He put his arm around her. "And where have you been?"

"I have been riding with Millicent . . . Lady Orville."

"And what did Lady Orville have to say for herself? Usually it is quite a bit."

"She is planning a dinner. She wants us to come."

"Ah, would you like to go, my dear?"

"Very much," she said. "I do enjoy her company."

"I am glad that you do. I have not seen Bruce—Lord Orville—for quite some time, and we have been friends since childhood."

"So she gave me to understand. Did you have a falling-out with him?"

"No, not precisely." He moved away from her and stood at a table flicking through the pages of a large book that was lying on top of it. "I am not criticizing Lady Orville, mind you. I know she is your friend, but Christina was never at ease with her. You must have noticed that she has a habit of saying exactly what she thinks, and she is also unsparingly frank. Christina did not appreciate this quality."

"Oh, really? I have noticed that she does believe in speaking her mind, true. But I enjoy knowing what people are thinking."

"Christina was exceptionally sensitive. It is possible

that she misunderstood Lady Orville."

"Perhaps she did. I do find her so very kind."

"If she has proved kind to you, my dear, I think I must revise my evaluation of her. It is possible that Christina did not take the trouble to know her. She never enjoyed going about in society. I am pleased that you do. We will have to give some dinners ourselves. I want you to become acquainted with some of the other families who live nearby. I think that among them you might find other young women who are quite as compatible as Lady Orville."

"I should enjoy meeting your friends," Laura said carefully. "And I think we should invite people here, do you not agree?"

He flicked through more pages of the volume on the table. "Yes indeed, it is high time that I ceased to be a hermit." Rather than looking at her, he kept his eyes on the book. "My sister has waxed very stern on the subject. And certainly she is right. You are both right. But now, my dear, if you will excuse me, I think I must inform the housekeeper concerning Mr. Quinn's arrival."

"Of course," Laura agreed. Once Eric had hurried out of the room, Laura, with a long sigh, sank down on an adjacent chair. Despite his acquiescence to her suggestion, she was, again, uncomfortably positive that she had, in effect, trespassed on forbidden ground. Eric did not really approve her friendship with Lady Orville because his wife had not liked her. He did not really approve her suggestion that they entertain his friends because Christina had not been a sociable person. Did he want her to follow in the lady's uncertain footsteps? She was sure he did not. Despite anything Eric could, and probably would, say to the contrary, he was not really her husband. He remained Christina's widower.

SIX

ON THEIR WAY TO LADY ORVILLE's dinner party, Eric, sitting beside Laura in the post chaise, broke a rather protracted silence by saying, "I am pleased that we are going, my dear."

"Are you?" she asked rather shyly.

"Yes, it is time that you met some of our other neighbors. I expect they have not left cards because of Christina's reticence. I am sure they judge me a recluse."

His comment surprised her. In the half a month she had been at his home—or, rather, "their home," as she must call it and try to expunge the feeling that she was an unwanted guest come for an indefinite state—Eric had made no reference to the lack of formal visits generally paid to a new arrival. Rather than giving him a direct answer, she contented herself with saying, "I expect they thought that since we were so recently wed . . ." She blushed, realizing that the observation she had been about to make, with its suggestion of a honeymoon, would be the last sort of a remark he would wish to hear.

"Yes, I can well imagine that they expected we would covet our privacy. Laura, my dear, you have been wonderfully forbearing. I . . ." He hesitated, for the carriage was slowing to a stop. "I forgot that the Orvilles live so near. I should not have forgotten. It will be good to see Bruce again."

"I imagine he will be pleased to see you too," Laura said. Eric was looking very handsome tonight. His evening clothes became him, and she found herself remembering the night they had met. He had looked similarly handsome. He had easily outshone all the gentlemen she had seen on that never-to-be-forgotten occasion, and again it seemed incredible that they should be married—especially after she had stepped on his toe.

He would suffer less were she to do it now, she thought with no little satisfaction. She had lost more weight, and this evening when she had come down to join him, he had commented on the change in her appearance. "You do look exceedingly lovely tonight, Laura, my dear," he had said on a note of surprise, and then he had fallen silent. She had wondered, and was still wondering, if he were comparing her to his lost love—but of course there could be no comparison.

More than ever she was convinced that he and his Christina had occupied an enchanted world of their own—one closed to all invasion, a Garden of Eden, or, better yet, a utopia. Then she remembered with a surge of excitement that Mr. Quinn had discovered an early edition of a Sir Thomas More work—dated 1530! She remembered the librarian, his eyes alight with excitement, as he had carefully shown her the thin, leatherbound volume. He had said wonderingly, "Just think, it was printed before Shakespeare was born, and he might easily have drawn upon it for *The Tempest.*" It was very pleasant to have Mr. Quinn in the house. He had made other discoveries in the library, and he was always eager to share them with her.

"My dear, whither are you wandering?" Eric said.

Laura looked up quickly and did not see him. "Where are . . ." she began confusedly.

"I am here, my dear, waiting to hand you down."

She realized then that the coach door had been opened, and rather than sitting beside her, Eric was standing by the steps waiting to hand her down. "Oh, dear, I was thinking," she told him.

"A most regrettable habit, and one that you must endeavor to conquer if you are to be like most females," he said lightly as he helped her out of the post chaise. "However, I might add that I, for one, find it singularly refreshing. In fact, your singularity in that regard was one of the reasons I married you. It is not every young woman who beguiles her time at Almack's with a book."

She looked up into his smiling face and felt a delicious warmth stealing over her. She had never seen so . . . dared she call his look ardent? She spoke over a pounding in her throat. "I have never tried to be like most females, Eric."

"I know," he said softly, "and that is what I most appreciate about you. Indeed, it occurs to me that I have never appreciated you enough. I have to believe that Lady Orville has proved far more discerning than myself."

Before Laura could reply, several other ladies and gentlemen moving in the direction of the castle had caught sight of Eric. There were delighted greetings and swift introductions, which Laura, meeting interested, curious, and pleased glances, feared she might not remember. Then they came into a large hall to be punctiliously announced by an elderly butler. Further introductions followed. Laura met a Lady Cavendish, a Lord Calvert, a Lieutenant Colonel Dashwood, Mr. and Mrs. James Lord, and Colonel Wiltshire with his lady, and hoped that she would have no difficulty in remembering them all.

Then suddenly Eric was separated from her by a tall, bronzed gentleman with a soldierly bearing, who later proved to be her host, Lord Bruce Orville. He told her that his lady was much taken with her but did not wait to hear her comment that she was fond of Lady Orville.

Indeed, there was a considerable amount of fractured conversation, of anecdotes told and interrupted by others who had been there at the time the said anecdote was in the process of unfolding. There was also a moment when her hostess determinedly dragged her into an alcove and said archly, "You are in such good looks tonight, my dear Laura. Am I to deduce . . . ?" She did not appear to be disappointed by Laura's embarrassed denials.

"The man is beginning to realize his errors, it is evident," she whispered. "And it is also time that Christina was drowned in a deep pool. She will be, after tonight. Bruce will have something to say about you. I have demanded that, and now that he has seen you, he is really quite annoyed with Eric—or I should be even more annoyed than he has been. I think he loathed Christina even more than myself. Husbands should be partial to their wives and allied against their enemies, my dear. Until the ghost is laid, Christina will be your enemy, but I feel that Eric is finally seeing the error of his ways."

"He *has* seemed different tonight," Laura murmured.

"And high time! He often watches you, you know. In fact, he is beginning to behave as a newly married man ought." Lady Orville winked. "I will hope that this behavior will be followed by other manly manifestations."

Laura blushed. "Millicent!" she protested.

"I know I am being outrageous, but also *he* is outrageous, and not so harmlessly, either. Sixteen days— shocking, I call it!"

Laura stared at her in horror. "I . . . I never told you that . . . that . . ."

"My love, that is part of it. Your reticence does you great credit, but it is also revealing to me, I who count myself your best friend. The man is a fool! I only hope that he will not come to appreciate you too late."

"Too late?" Laura repeated, staring at Lady Orville incredulously.

"Oh, Laura, Laura, Laura, I could shake you," Lady Orville hissed. "At a word, you would lie down and let him walk on you, and it should be the other way around.

There, I will say no more, because you will not understand and you will be unhappy, and I have invited you here so that our neighbors and friends can see what an excellent choice your husband has made. I also hope that Eric, who has been looking your way while we have been conversing—or, rather, while I have been conversing—will see the error of his ways and cease these sins of omission."

Having had her say, Lady Orville left Laura's side, and her position was usurped by other ladies. Everyone appeared to like her, and as the evening ended, she felt happy and excited. Despite her lingering shyness, she had enjoyed herself, and Eric appeared in high good humor as he handed her into the post chaise.

"My dear," he said, pulling her against him, "you have made an excellent impression."

"Did I?" Laura asked, thinking only of the warmth of his arm on her shoulders, and the warmth of his tone as well.

"You seem to have had no trouble conversing with anyone. Bruce remarked on it. It was good seeing him again."

"I should imagine you would have, since your estates adjoin each other. I hope that you had a chance to speak with Lady Orville."

"I did, and I found her charming."

"Oh, I am pleased. You do like her, then?"

"I think I like her mainly because she seems to like you, and consequently shows excellent taste." Eric bent to kiss her. The kiss might have begun by being casual, but it lasted a surprisingly long time. "Laura, my dearest Laura," he said finally, "what a damned fool I have been!"

"Oh, n-no—" she began.

"Oh, yes," he interrupted. "And I do hope that you will forgive . . ." He paused, for the post chaise had traversed the relatively short distance that lay between the two estates and was rolling into the stable yard. Though it was dark, there was a full moon that night, and

standing in a bright pool of moonlight was a wraithlike
figure clad in white and wringing its hands.

As Eric, usurping the place of his footman,
wonderingly helped Laura from the coach, the figure ran
toward them, wailing, "Oh, where have you been? You
must help me, Laura, I have left my husband and I . . . I
do not know what to do." However, it was not to Laura
that Julia turned. She flung herself into her brother-in-
law's arms and sobbed against him as if her heart would
break.

Eric stared down at Julia incredulously. Even in her
agony, her moon-illuminated features bore a startling
resemblance to Christina. Automatically his arms tightened around her quivering body. He said gently, protec-
tively, "My poor child, what is amiss?"

"I . . . I . . ." Julia looked up at him piteously, and
then, upon receiving the support of his arms, her last bit
of strength appeared to ebb and she swooned.

"I must get her inside," he said unnecessarily.

"Yes," Laura agreed faintly, thinking . . . but she did
not know what to think, could not think at such a time.
Julia must be brought into the house, and Eric had easily
lifted her and was carrying her inside. At this hour the
servants had retired, save for her abigail, Eric's valet, and
the footman who had admitted them.

Fortunately Lucy could make the bed in one of the
many spare rooms, but Eric, still encumbered by his fair
burden, directed that Julia be put in the chamber his
sister had once occupied, it being more commodious and
better furnished than the others. Furthermore, it was
close to the suite that he and Laura occupied.

Laura, trailing behind him, watched as he brought
Julia into the chamber, his voice edgy as he directed
Lucy to hurry. Then he carefully put Julia on the chaise
longue, and in the glow of a hastily lighted candelabra
he scanned her unconscious face.

"She is so very pale," he said anxiously.

Julia was always pale. She had very little color in her
cheeks. Laura longed to provide that information but

could not. Shock and fear had put a bridle on her tongue, and there was agony as well. In a moment that seemingly had held great promise, when her husband had seemed more interested, more caring—if not actually loving—her sister Julia, like a bird of ill omen, had come to dispel her happiness again—and now what would happen?

Conjecture was beyond her. She could not consider the ramifications attendant upon Julia's arrival. She must minister to her stricken sister, or else be thought uncaring and even inhuman. She came to stand near Eric at the chaise longue.

"Should we not apply burned feathers?" she suggested.

"Beggin' your pardon, milady," Lucy said crisply as she slid pillows into their cases, "but my sister's much given to faintin' fits, and water splashed in 'er face brings 'er about quick as that."

"Water, then?" Laura suggested.

"Yes," Eric agreed. "Lucy, will you fetch some . . ." He paused as Julia stirred and moaned. "Never mind," he added quickly. "I believe she is . . . recovering."

Julia opened her eyes, and staring fearfully into Eric's anxious face, she wailed, "Oh, p-please, he . . . he must not find me."

"My poor, poor child, what has happened?" he asked solicitously and tenderly and in a tone Laura had never heard from him before.

"Oh, E-Eric, it is you," Julia said wonderingly. "But . . . but how did I . . . I get here? I . . . I am so confused!"

"I brought you, my dear. You are in my sister's chamber, and you are quite safe with us," Eric assured her gently.

"Am I?" Julia shuddered. "Am I safe anywhere as long as *he* remains in the world? Oh, God, God, God, I have lived in such stultifying terror that I scarcely know the meaning of the word *safe*. Am . . . am I really safe? If he should come searching for m-me . . . ." Julia shuddered again.

"If he should come here, my dear, he will have me to

deal with," Eric said soothingly. "I assure you, you will
have nothing to fear from him in this house. You are with
me."

Us. He should have said *us,* something in Laura's
half-benumbed mind informed her, but he had not. She
was seized by a most frightening sensation. She felt as if
the room had suddenly narrowed to exclude her, leaving
only the two of them, Eric and Julia, staring into each
other's eyes. Were she to leave, she was positive that Eric
would not even notice her departure, for it was not
Julia's face that was looking back at him from the
pillows—it was that of Christina, to whom she bore so
fatal a resemblance. Acting on that same conviction,
Laura moved out of the room and went down the hall to
her own chamber. Out of habit she looked about for Lucy
and belatedly remembered that the abigail was making
Julia's bed. Usually she would have undressed, but this
gown was complicated, and she must needs wait, as she
had often waited in the days when she and Julia had
shared an abigail.

Later, when a taciturn Lucy had helped her mistress
undress, bade her good night, and gone up to her room
on the third floor, Laura, lying in her wide bed, remembered Eric's words and the warmth of his arms around
her on the way home—as well as the promise she had
believed they held. She wondered if after leaving Julia he
might come to her chamber, if only to bid her good night,
but she was almost positive that he would not.

By the time the clock struck one in the morning,
Laura, being truly positive that Eric would not come,
ceased to contend against a determined Morpheus and
fell asleep.

Informed that Lady Orville had arrived and was now
awaiting her hostess in the drawing room, Laura, in the
library, discussing a rare edition of Percy's *Reliques*
dated 1765 with Mr. Quinn, flushed and wished she
dared say that she was not at home. Unfortunately she
could not issue such a rebuff to dear Millicent, even

though in the last week she had declared herself not at home to those visitors who, having met her on the night of Lady Orville's dinner, had sent cards.

She had also declined an invitation from one Lady Kirwan, whom she vaguely remembered as having sat next to her at the dinner. Lady Kirwan had invited Lord and Lady Marne to attend a gathering in her gardens, which, Laura had heard, were famous. She had not even communicated Lady Kirwan's wishes to Eric, for she knew full well that he would not have wanted to attend.

Upon Julia's recovery from her husband's brutal assault, evident in the angry discoloration of her upper arm and in the swelling of one delicate wrist which her enraged spouse had twisted, nearly breaking the bone, Eric had assigned himself the task of being Julia's unofficial physician and official comforter. He had spent a great deal of time in her chamber, reading to her and otherwise soothing her lacerated feelings.

On the third day after her arrival, Julia had pronounced herself well enough to rise from her bed. Eric had obligingly carried her down to the conservatory. Julia had pronounced the rare plants much to her liking, and indeed had contrived to amaze Laura by telling him that she, too, had a passion for gardening and was particularly fond of the rare blooms that the late Lady Christina had collected.

However, when Laura had attempted to find out what her brother-in-law had done to send Julia flying from the house, she had waxed hysterical again, and an angered Eric had scolded Laura for needlessly distressing her frail sister. He had sought to alleviate the damage her thoughtlessness had engendered by taking the invalid for a long drive in his curricle. Then, on the following day, when Julia had told him that she was feeling much more the thing, he had taken her to Glastonbury. The visit had lasted all of the day, after which Julia had pronounced herself too weary to undertake the journey back to the castle. A footman had been dispatched to Laura, explaining the circumstances and assuring her that her husband

and her sister would be returning the following afternoon.

As it happened, they had not returned on that designated afternoon. They had returned mid-morning of the next day, blaming a broken wheel on the coach, which had necessitated a return to Glastonbury. Julia had been full of apologies and praise. The praise had been divided equally between the kindness of her dear, considerate brother-in-law and the charm of the town. In common with herself and Eric, they had gone to the George and Pilgrim, whence they returned to stay the night. Julia had woken her brother-in-law in the middle of the night with the quavering announcement that she had seen the ghostly monk. He had spent the rest of the night sitting on a chair in her chamber, lest the specter return again, Julia had told Laura in tones of awe and gratitude, her eyes wide with surprise because she had never known a gentleman to be so very considerate. She further complimented Laura, saying that she had made the best marriage in the family!

On this day Julia and Eric were bound for Bridgewater Bay, Julia having expressed a hankering to view the sea. Laura grimaced. Eric had seemed embarrassed and even reluctant to accede to his sister-in-law's request. The time was approaching for the festivities attendant upon the Eve of St. John, and in an expansive moment he had invited Lord and Lady Orville to attend and had also asked several other persons present at that never-to-be-forgotten dinner.

Laura had dutifully written the invitations. She had also overseen preparations which, in ordinary circumstances, must have been allocated to her husband. However, a gently persuasive and wistful Julia had prevailed, as she always must. They had left early in the morning.

Consequently Laura, with the events of the last week whirling through her mind, said reluctantly to the waiting servant, "You may inform her ladyship that I will be there directly." She bestowed a warm smile on Mr. Quinn. "I do thank you for bringing this volume to my attention. I do love old ballads."

"As I do myself, my lady," he said.

A few minutes later Laura came into the drawing room but did not find her ladyship. Then Tim, one of the footmen, came to inform her that her ladyship was in the garden by the fish pond.

As she arrived at the pool Laura found her friend staring into its dark green waters on which floated lily pads and other aquatic plants. On exchanging greetings and an embrace with Laura, Lady Orville said, "I expect there are carp in this pond, but they are proving to be as elusive as you, my dear. Do you suppose that they, in common with yourself, are beset by a visiting sister?"

Laura blushed. "I am sorry that we have not met recently, but these last few days have been extremely hectic."

"Yes, I understand that your sister recovered rather quickly from whatever ailed her at the time of her arrival, and that she has been much in the company of her brother-in-law, who is endeavoring to ease the distress she has endured at the hands of an Othello-like spouse—by showing her some of the felicitous spots around the countryside. They are currently in Bridgewater, I hear."

Laura gaped at her. "How . . ." she began faintly.

"My dear love, the servants, of course," Lady Orville explained. "They know everything—as I think I told you some time ago. I believe that they engage in those marathons so popular in ancient Greece, save that instead of passing on a torch, they substitute information."

Laura said, "Julia was very badly treated by her husband, and Eric was much exercised over the matter. He has felt it incumbent upon himself to be kind to her."

"Hmm." Lady Orville grimaced. "Evidently he has not yet learned that it is quite useless to be kind to crocodiles. Ply them with meat from a distance. If you get too close to them, they would as lief take your hand with the meat. I am quite annoyed with you, Laura. Why have you not sent Julia on to your mother? That is the usual destination for a battered bride."

"I did suggest that she go to Mother, but Eric was quite indignant and asked me if I could not see that she was in no condition to travel."

"How did she get from Cornwall to Somerset? On the back of an eagle, perchance? Or perhaps she hired a balloon."

"She came by post-chaise. She was ill on the way."

"However," Lady Orville responded caustically, "the air of Somerset being more healthful than the sea winds that drift over Land's End, she recovered her health, thus giving the lie to those who tout the curable quotient in a sea breeze. Are you so utterly naive, Laura, or have you like the turtle learned to draw your head into your shell and remain oblivious to danger, if not actually protected against it? I understand that a turtle is quite helpless if turned on its back. If you do not watch yourself, my dear, that will be your charming sister's next move."

Laura said unhappily, "She does resemble Christina. I expect that must be extremely unsettling to Eric."

"Something of which I am sure your sister is completely aware. Oh!" Lady Orville stamped her foot and glared at Laura. "I could shake you, my dear. Are you going to stand idly by while that little witch . . . oh, my poor child," she said in a softer tone as, coming to Laura's chair, she bent down and put her arms around her. "I do wish you were not so vulnerable, so much in awe of your wretched sister, who thrives on making you miserable because of her own selfish needs."

"Her needs?" Laura repeated confusedly.

"Do you not see?" Lady Orville cried angrily. "Without even knowing her I can guess what she is like. She feeds on admiration, adulation, and adoration. If she cannot find them at home, she will seek them elsewhere, and most determinedly. They are the fuel that lights her fires. She could not exist without them, and since she can give so very little in return, she must constantly seek for new sources. I have a strong feeling that she does not wear well, my dear Laura. Her husband was cruel to her? Probably he finally probed her depths and found no more than an inch of water in the pond. Consequently she must seek for others who do not realize that beneath that beautiful reflection on the surface of that same pond, there are only weeds beneath."

Almost against her will, Laura laughed. She sobered quickly enough. "I do not believe that Eric would agree with you."

"Damn all women who die too young," Lady Orville said in exasperated tones. Then, with her habitual abruptness, she added, "How is the librarian progressing?"

"Mr. Quinn is most knowledgeable. He has found some real treasures," Laura said enthusiastically, glad to be diverted from the unhappy topic of her infatuated husband and her beguiling sister.

Fortunately for her further peace of mind, Lady Orville, after listening patiently to the number of marvels Mr. Quinn had exhumed from the library archives, took her leave. Her parting words were, "Since you are disposed to do nothing about Julia, I will pray for a deus ex machina—possibly Zeus to come in his flaming chariot to rid you of her just when matters appear to be at the very worst."

"I will pray too," Laura heard herself reply, much to her subsequent embarrassment. "I mean . . ." she began hastily.

"If you do not mean exactly what I hope you mean, you are no friend of mine," Lady Orville replied with her usual candor. "I will see you the day after tomorrow, and at what time will you be lighting the fires?"

"You may come at any time, but the fires will be lighted after sundown."

"Let us pray that they will do as they are supposed to do, which is to avert disaster and bring luck. You need both, my dearest Laura."

"The midsummer fires are a pagan survival," Mr. Quinn remarked, as in company with Laura, Julia, and the Orvilles, they strolled down the hill in the direction of the keep where a huge pile of kindling wood, gathered by the gardeners on the previous day, stood ready to be ignited.

"A pagan survival, really?" Julia asked. She laughed lightly. "That would be dating from the time when the early Britons painted themselves blue, I expect. I am glad that custom did not survive. What an odd idea, to be sure!"

"I would think it no more odd than some of the exaggerated garments that are worn today by the dandies." Mr. Quinn smiled.

"Oh, indeed?" Julia gave him a chilly stare. "Are you setting yourself up to be an arbiter of fashion, then, Mr. Quinn?" She let her eyes rest on his shabby garments.

"Julia!" Laura protested. "Mr. Quinn was doing nothing of the kind, and some of the garments that are affected by gentlemen are ridiculous. What about that odd creature—I do not remember his name—who chooses to wear nothing but green and eats only green food?"

"And what about neck cloths that keep the chin tilted at an unnatural angle, preventing the wearer from looking down? I have heard it said that many a dandy has sustained a serious fall, and deserved it too." Lord Orville appeared to shudder. "I am of the opinion that garments must be comfortable first and stylish second."

"Precisely, my love," his lady agreed. "It is the way I wish to live my entire life."

"And have," her husband said impishly. Putting his arm around her waist, he gave her a loving little squeeze.

Julia visited a chilly glance on Lord and Lady Orville. Then, turning to Laura, she said, "When will Eric be lighting the fire? It is getting quite dark."

"I expect he is waiting until we arrive," Laura said, thinking that he was probably waiting until Julia arrived. "Gracious!" she exclaimed as they approached the keep. "I did not think they would make three piles of wood . . . and they are so high.

"Three is a mystical number," Mr. Quinn observed.

"Yes." Lord Orville nodded. "And generally the piles are as high as those and even higher."

"There is quite a little wind tonight," Laura said worriedly. "Do you think it safe?"

"The keep will act as a windbreak," Lord Orville said soothingly.

"It is like you to fret over nothing, Laura." Julia laughed. Before her sister could answer, she added, "It bids fair to be a lovely evening." She held up her arms. "Night's candles are all aglow, some poet has said."

"He has said," Lady Orville corrected, " 'night's candles are all burnt out and jocund day stands tiptoe on the misty mountaintops.' He has also said, 'oh, grim-locked night, oh, night with hue so black, oh, night which ever are when day is not, oh, night, oh, night, alack, alack, alack.' "

"Millicent . . ." Her husband groaned.

He received a mischievous smile as Lady Orville said, "I am following Lady Ludlow's lead and quoting the bard, do you not like it? I have always been particularly partial to *A Midsummer Night's Dream,* and certainly it is an apt quotation for this particular midsummer's night," she responded challengingly.

All she received by way of response from her lord was a raised eyebrow, and subsequently a glare from Julia, who moved swiftly ahead of them.

A few minutes later the small group of people, with Julia still in the lead, reached the keep, its time and war-scored lineaments softened in the glow from a three-quarter moon over which pale clouds drifted. In the west, a faint and fading line of red still remained.

"Oh, how beautiful," Laura said softly. "Ah, there are the servants," she added as a babble of conversation reached them.

"My dear Laura, why are *they* here?" Julia asked disapprovingly.

"Because Eric gave them leave to watch the lighting of the bonfires. It is a tradition here," Laura explained. "Did he not tell you?"

"We did not discuss the event, Laura, dear," Julia murmured, her meaning all too clear. She added quickly, "Where is Eric?"

"He is probably having his torch lighted so that he might ignite the fires," Lady Orville explained, indicating the three piles of timber.

"He will ignite the middle one first, I understand." Laura frowned. "I hope the blaze will not frighten his horse."

"Dear Laura, always borrowing trouble," Julia said with a little laugh.

"It does not usually catch on so quickly," Lord Orville assured Laura.

"Ah, look," Julia cried a few minutes later, "the sunlight has faded completely! It should be time and here he comes! Does he not sit that great black horse like Launcelot himself?"

"Yes, very like Launcelot, himself," Lady Orville said so dryly that even though she was not in the mood for laughter, Laura could not restrain a giggle.

In that moment Eric rode forward to fling his torch upon the middle pile, and of a sudden there was a puff of wind and a burst of flame which seemed to envelop horse and rider. With a neigh that bordered on a shriek, the stallion reared, unseating its rider and dashing away—the while Eric, thrown heavily to the ground, lay very still.

Julia screamed and started toward him, but it was Laura who reached him first, kneeling beside him and easing his head onto her lap.

There were great cries and a babble of comment from the assembled observers, and then Lord Orville, reaching Laura's side, said urgently, "We must get him home." He looked about him, and seeing a servant, he yelled, "Bring a plank . . . a door, if you can find one."

As the man nodded and dashed away, Julia, standing just beyond Laura, began to cry. "Is . . . is he dead? Oh, God, he cannot be dead!"

The librarian, who, all but unnoticed by Julia and Laura, had come to Eric's side, now knelt beside him.

"He is not dead. He is breathing, but"—he frowned—"I think a doctor must be summoned immediately."

"Can a doctor help him?" Julia wailed. "He lies so still."

"I beg you will stop shrieking and make an effort to contain yourself," Lady Orville said icily. "We none of us know anything, and will not until the doctor arrives."

"His face . . ." Julia shuddered. "It is so red. He must have been burned."

"I believe that he was singed by the flames." Lord Orville frowned. "And it is possible, judging from the angle of his leg, that he has broken a bone. His ankle is also swelling."

"Oh, God." Julia wrung her hands. She moved to Laura's side. "I must be with him. He will want me."

"On the contrary, Lady Ludlow," Lady Orville snapped. "I am sure that were he conscious, he would prefer the less hysterical ministrations of his wife."

Julia whirled on her and seemed on the point of delivering a sharp retort, but meeting Lady Orville's cool stare, she appeared to think better of it and instead came to stand near her kneeling sister. "How . . . how is he?" she said, quavering.

Laura shook her head. "He . . . he is still unconscious." She looked anxiously about her. "I do wish they would hurry with that plank. We must get him to his chamber."

"Yes, yes, of course," Julia agreed. "He cannot lie out here. Oh, dear, why did this have to happen?"

"I would imagine," said a chilly voice behind her, "that he rode too close to the flames, and fire is inimical to both men and moths."

Julia whirled on the speaker, who of course was Lady Orville. "I find your wit sadly misplaced at such a time."

"Indeed? And what has caused you to imagine that I was being witty?" Lady Orville retorted. "I had the impression that I was saying no more than the truth."

Julia was prevented from uttering the sharp rejoinder that trembled on her tongue by the two men from the castle, who came carrying an old door, which they set beside the fallen man. Under Laura's directions they gently eased him onto it, and in a few minutes they started back to the castle, followed by Laura, Lord and Lady Orville, Mr. Quinn, and an increasingly distracted Julia.

By the time Eric had been brought into his chamber and put to bed by his concerned and nervous valet, the doctor arrived, and after requesting more light, he curtly ordered everyone out of the room.

As Laura, Julia, and Lord and Lady Orville moved into the adjacent sitting room, Laura sank down in a chair, and the Orvilles sat on a nearby sofa. Julia, pacing back and forth across the room, looked at them in angry amazement. "How can you be so c-calm?" she cried, her accusing glance falling on Laura's face. "He . . . he has been badly hurt, I am sure of it."

"I am not sure of it," Lady Orville responded coldly. "I will reserve my fears until the doctor gives us his opinion."

"But surely you . . . you saw—" Julia began.

"Julia," Laura interrupted softly. "It is useless to conjecture. We must wait until Mr. Chatterton finishes his examination."

"If . . . if it were my husband, I would not leave his side, not for an instant!" Julia cried.

"But your husband is in Cornwall, is he not?" Lady Orville inquired.

"Just what are you implying?" Julia demanded angrily.

"I was not implying anything," Lady Orville responded serenely. "I was merely stating what your sister led me to believe was the truth."

"My love . . ." Lord Orville muttered warningly.

"My . . . my husband was uncommonly cruel to me," Julia said in a quavering voice. "It . . . it was for my own safety that I fled. Laura knows and understands my plight."

"I am sure she does," Lady Orville said sweetly.

"Millicent!" her husband hissed.

"If you imagine . . ." Julia began, and paused as the

door to Eric's chamber was opened by Mr. Chatterton, a tall, portly man who said in a low voice, "Lady Marne, would you please come in?"

"Is he awake, then?" Julia cried as Laura, rising swiftly, hurried toward the door to the inner room.

"No." The doctor shook his head. "I have given him a dose of laudanum. It will quell his pain, at least for a little while."

"Is he in much pain?" Julia demanded hysterically as she started to follow Laura.

"His eyes . . ." the doctor began.

"Oh, God, you will not tell me that he . . . he has been blinded!" Julia shrieked.

"Will you have the goodness to be quiet?" Lady Orville rose and confronted Julia, standing between her and the door.

"How dare you?" Julia cried as Laura went inside, followed by the doctor, who swiftly closed the door behind him.

"It is Laura's place to be with her husband, and none other," Lady Orville said pointedly. "She is his wife."

"But he . . . but we . . ." Julia blurted.

"Yes, I know." Lady Orville nodded. "But not at this time. I suggest that you return to your seat and, better yet, to Cornwall, Lady Ludlow."

"Millicent!" Lord Orville groaned.

"My dear Bruce," his wife said coldly, "I hardly think that at this time poor Laura is in need of houseguests."

Julia glared at her. "I must say that you take a great deal on yourself, Lady Orville."

"I am your sister's friend," the latter responded pointedly.

"I . . . you . . ." Julia glared at her and left the room.

"Ah." Lady Orville favored her husband with a triumphant smile. "Let us hope that she will soon go home."

"Yes, do let us hope that she will, my dear, but all the same, you do walk in where angels fear to tread." Lord Orville gave her a half-censorious, half-admiring look.

"I am no angel." Lady Orville permitted herself a

small smile, which faded immediately. "That wretched young woman! I wish it had been her on the horse, and I wish he had tossed her into the flames!"

"My dear," her husband protested. "Evil intentions . . ."

"'Evil intentions return to plague the inventor.' Shakespeare again, and those lines do not apply to me. If anyone were ever evil-intentioned, it is that creature. I used to be sorry that I did not have sisters. I am not sorry anymore."

"The mills of the gods grind slowly . . ." Lord Orville began.

"Too damned slowly," Lady Orville snapped, and was silent, staring anxiously at the door. "It is time that Julia paid the piper. I am sure it was she who egged poor Eric on to lighting that bonfire on horseback."

"Now, Millicent, my love, you know full well that is a tradition here."

"If it is, it should be 'more honored in the breach than in the observance.'"

"I am quite in agreement, my dear. I only hope . . ."

"Yes," Lady Orville said grimly. "So do I."

A short time later Laura came out, followed by the doctor, who was finishing some directives. "The compresses must be applied three times a day—good, hot water. I have set his leg, and I would not worry too much about his ankle. It is not broken, it is only a bad sprain."

"Will he take long to recover, Mr. Chatterton?" Laura asked anxiously.

"I cannot predict that, milady, but he is young and healthy, and fortunately the bone did not shatter. He suffered a clean break of the tibia. I have bound it, and I would think that in two or three months he will be quite himself again. His ankle, of course, should heal more quickly. You must see that it, too, is soaked in warm water three times a day and kept tightly bandaged."

"His . . . his eyes . . ." Laura began in a voice that was not quite steady.

"You need follow my directives and apply the compresses. Keep him in a darkened room. I would think that in a matter of four to five weeks they will have healed. Again, he is young and healthy and not given to overindulgence either at table or the bottle. He will, of course, require careful nursing." The doctor grimaced. "In view of what is available here in the way of nursing . . ."

"I will see that he is well tended, sir," Laura assured him.

"I am sure you will, milady." Mr. Chatterton gave her an admiring look. "I must congratulate you on your admirable good sense in not revealing your anxiety while in the presence of the patient."

"I did not wish to alarm him," Laura said.

"You are quite right. He must be kept as calm as possible."

"I will see that he is, Mr. Chatterton." Laura said.

"Then I will bid you good evening, milady."

"Good evening, sir, and I am grateful that you came as quickly as you did."

"I would always come in haste, milady. Your husband and his family have been my patients for a number of years. And I beg you will not worry—as long as my directions are followed, he will mend easily. He needs only to be kept quiet and reassured as to his eventual recovery."

"He shall be," Laura assured him.

"I pray that you will take the doctor's directives to heart, dearest Laura," Lady Orville said shortly after the doctor had gone. "I take it that Eric is awake."

"Yes," Laura said. "I will have to return to him soon. He is naturally anxious and in some pain. The doctor has administered laudanum, but it has not yet taken effect."

"Yes, certainly you must go back to him. We only lingered to hear what Mr. Chatterton would say. We will go immediately," Lady Orville assured her.

"I . . . I do thank you, Millicent. You have been kind," Laura murmured.

"My dear, you need not thank us. We are friends,

friends of yourself and poor Eric. And though it is quite useless to offer you advice, I would suggest that you do not spend all the night and all the day at your husband's side. Let others minister to him as well."

Laura nodded. "Yes," she said, wishing that her friend would leave.

"See us to the door, my dear"—Lady Orville smiled—"and we will do your bidding."

Laura regarded her confusedly, "My bidding? I do not understand you."

Lord Orville laughed. "My wife believes that you wish her to go—and quickly, as do I."

"Oh, no, b-but . . ."

"But I would wish the same were anything to happen to dear Bruce, I can assure you," Lady Orville assured her warmly. "I will expect you to keep us informed as to his condition, my dear."

"Oh, I will," Laura nodded. "Where is Julia? Eric has been calling for her."

"I imagine that she is in her chamber," Lady Orville said coolly. "She seemed on the edge of the vapors, and I did not believe that she should treat either you or your husband to such a display at this time. I fear that I told her as much."

"Oh, I am glad that you did!" Laura exclaimed. "Julia is prone to the vapors."

"I also suggested that she return to Cornwall," Lady Orville said. "I hope you will do the same. Or, if not that, to your mother's house. Either would be a *logical* destination."

Laura regarded her unhappily. "In Eric's present condition it might be better were she to remain. Mr. Chatterton said that he should be kept as calm as possible."

"And you believe that Julia would have a calming effect on him?" Lady Orville demanded caustically.

"My dear . . ." Lord Orville began.

Laura said doggedly, "He appears to like her. I think he would be disappointed were she to leave."

"And I think you ought to change your name to Patient Griselda!" Lady Orville snapped.

"My dear . . ." Lord Orville protested.

Tears stood in Laura's eyes and were determinedly blinked away. "I am *not* a Griselda," she said with an actual stamp of her foot. "It is that the doctor said he must not be disturbed, and I happen to believe that Julia's abrupt departure *would* prove very disturbing to him. She will probably not remain here very long. Indeed, she will undoubtedly leave of her own accord within the week."

"That seems logical," Lady Orville said dryly. "She . . . but no matter, you know my opinion regarding your sister, my dear."

"I am sure she does," Lord Orville said wryly. "You have certainly made no secret of it, my love."

"Were I to be as silent as the tomb, Julia's own actions would furnish the corroboration I require. But enough. We will leave you. I will speak to you in a day or two regarding Eric's condition, though judging from what Mr. Chatterton has said, he is in little danger."

"I do thank you," Laura said. "I will see you to the door."

"No, see us only to the top of the stairs," Lady Orville replied. "We will have no trouble finding our way out."

Having done as Lady Orville asked, Laura hurried back in the direction of Eric's chamber, coming to a dead stop in the hallway as Julia emerged from the door in question. She was looking less concerned than angry.

"He is asleep," she said accusingly. "I could not rouse him, though I called his name quite loudly."

Laura quelled a rising anger only with difficulty. She said coolly, "Why would you want to wake him, Julia? It is better that he sleep. That is what the doctor told me."

"I am sure that he would have wanted to bid me farewell," Julia said crossly. "I will be leaving first thing in the morning. I have asked the stable boys to see that my post chaise is in good order. I am going to London to stay with Lady Grosvenor. We were best friends at school, and she has been wanting me to visit her for an age."

Caught between concern and relief, Laura said, "But will you not wait to speak to Eric? I am sure he would want to wish you farewell."

"I think not," Julia said coldly. "And you need not resort to any further subterfuges. I am quite aware that it was you who asked Lady Orville to speak to me in that horrid way. If you wished me to go, you had only to tell me so—straight out. If there is anything I cannot abide, it is deceit."

"But I assure you, Julia, I said nothing to Lady Orville," Laura began earnestly.

Julia drew herself up. "Please, I pray you will not resort to further prevarication. I am quite aware that you deeply resented the friendship between your unfortunate husband and myself. And since above all things I wish to avoid any further unpleasantness of the nature I suffered before I was forced to flee my home, I will leave him to your tender mercies, Laura."

"I expect that you mean, Julia, that you do not find my husband quite as fascinating now that he is ill and unable to squire you about," Laura said coolly.

Julia glared at her. "On the contrary, Laura, dear, if there is anything that I abominate, it is envy and jealousy, and you have been demonstrating both in ever-increasing proportions. Furthermore . . . but I have already expressed myself on this regrettable situation, and I trust I need say nothing more."

"You are quite right, Julia, you need say nothing more," Laura responded equably. "And now, if you will excuse me, I think I must go to my husband."

"I do wish you joy of him," Julia said spitefully.

"I have had great joy from him," Laura could not help responding.

"Really?" Julia drawled. "That is not the impression I received from him. But you were always rather obtuse, were you not, Laura? Mama has often told me that she wondered at your lack of sensitivity." Turning her back on her, Julia walked away.

Of course she had invited such a response, Laura reasoned, but had Eric really confided his unhappiness with a marriage to which he had agreed mainly because of his need for an heir—to her sister? That did not seem likely, but how could she be sure? she thought unhappily. Eric had certainly spent a great deal of time with Julia, and undoubtedly those hours had not passed in silence.

She did not acquit her sister of complaining loudly and lengthily about her unhappy marriage to a sympathetic Eric. Had he responded with a spate of similar complaints in regards to his own? It was not beyond the realm of possibility—especially given Julia's uncanny resemblance to his late, beloved Christina. Possessing those attributes plus her own beauty, Julia was certainly a formidable rival, but, Laura thought with a surge of happiness, she *was* leaving.

A few minutes later, coming into Eric's chamber, Laura tiptoed to his side and started to sit down, but unfortunately she passed too close to the table and something crashed to the floor.

"W-who is it? Who is there?" Eric questioned in a trembling voice as he tried to sit up.

"It is only I, my love," Laura said softly. She put a gentle but firm hand on his shoulder. "Do lie back, my dearest. Mr. Chatterton has said that you must lie very still."

"Oh, Julia, my dear," Eric said happily, "I was wondering if you would come."

Laura stepped back from the bed. Her heart was pounding in her throat again. It was on the tip of her tongue to enlighten him. But at the same time she was truly angry with herself for not identifying herself immediately. Unfortunately she had quite forgotten the one characteristic that she shared with her beautiful sister, the characteristic that had even confused and startled her mother—that soft, slightly husky voice which was so entirely beguiling when it issued from Julia's lovely lips. She opened her mouth on a hasty denial and hastily swallowed it. She said instead, "But, Eric, dear, you knew I must."

SEVEN

"All Kings and all their favorites,
  All glory of honors, beauties, wits,
  The sun, itself, which makes times, as they
        pass.
  Is elder by a year now, than it was
  When thou and I first one another saw.
  All other things to their destruction draw.
  Only their love hath no decay,
  This, no tomorrow hath, nor yesterday,
  Running, it never runs from us away.
  But truly keeps his first, last everlasting day."

"HOW BEAUTIFULLY YOU READ THAT, Julia. Donne is a
favorite of mine. How did you guess that?"

"I am afraid that I did not guess that, Eric. Mr. Quinn
showed me the volume, which he said was very old—
published in the poet's lifetime, fancy! I chose the poem
because it is one of my favorites too."

"Ah, our tastes are amazingly alike."

"So it would appear, Eric."

"And yet Laura once told me that you were not much
of a reader."

"I am not much of a reader by Laura's standards. She

reads a great deal more than I. Generally I have very little time to settle down with a book. I am always grateful for the diversion when I have a quiet hour or two."

"I expect that Mr. Quinn has proved helpful?"

"I find him very helpful. Laura has praised him highly too."

"Laura, yes," Eric said rather uncomfortably. "Does she spend a great deal of time in the library?"

"When she is not here with you or riding. Horses and books, those are Laura's two greatest passions. Of course, that is understandable. My sister does not like to sew . . . but why must we discuss Laura? She is so very dull!"

Eric moved restlessly and frowned. "I would prefer you not to criticize Laura, Julia."

"Oh?" The woman by the bed rose. "I will fetch her, then, if you wish."

"Hold," he protested. "I did not say I wished you to fetch her. I . . . I look forward to your visits. Indeed, it is deadly dull for me when you are not here. Please, my dear, do stay with me a little longer."

"Very well, but if you would prefer Laura to come . . ."

"I would not prefer Laura to come, Julia. You know that I . . . I enjoy your company. And you are uncommonly kind to spend so much time with me. I thought you must have gone at least a week ago."

"I should have gone. Fancy, I have been here ten days!"

"I know, and I am so grateful that you have stayed, my dear."

"I should have gone, but I . . . I did not want to leave you. Oh, dear, I should not have said that."

"No." A brief smile played about Eric's lips. "You should not have said that, and I should not have been so pleased that you did."

"Eric!"

"Have I shocked you?"

"Well," she said hesitantly, "neither of us is—"

"I know," he interrupted hastily. "I hope Laura is not disturbed at the amount of time you spend with me."

"She has not said much about it. As I have told you, she rides a great deal and reads . . . but of course she has spent some time in here."

"But more in the library with Mr. Quinn, I believe. Should I be jealous of Mr. Quinn?" He smiled.

"I hardly think so, Eric. She is also conferring with the housekeeper. She wants to make some changes in the house . . . re-covering of the chairs and so on."

"Does she?" He frowned.

"Has she not discussed that with you?"

"If she has, I do not remember."

"You're frowning. Do you not approve of changes?"

He hesitated. "I expect some of the furnishings are very shabby. Nothing much has been done to the house since my mother's time. Christina was more interested in her gardens and woods. Yes, I think it would be well were Laura to make some changes. After all, it is her home now."

"I will tell her what you have said. I am sure she will be pleased."

"No, Julia, I think you had best let me tell her. Poor Laura." He sighed. "I am afraid I have not been quite fair with her."

"Nor I."

"No, you have not, Julia, but I am pleased that you no longer criticize her as you once did. I should not have listened to you, you know. I should have defended her."

"I have the impression that you are scolding me, Eric."

"I am a little, and scolding myself as well."

"I think I had better go."

"No, please . . . not yet." Eric reached out his hand, groping for her.

She quickly caught his hand, holding it gently. "Very well, I will stay a little longer."

"Please, Julia . . . you will have to go—and soon, I expect. London beckons, and surely I am a poor alternative."

"If you are going to say such things, I will go immediately. I do not like you in these humble moods, Eric."

"There's where you differ from Christina."

"Oh? Are you saying that I do not differ greatly from her in other ways?"

"You are amazingly alike," he said slowly. "Save that I doubt that she would have been so patient with my illness."

"You are saying, in effect, that she lacked sympathy?"

"She did not lack it . . . but so much of her day was spent among her plants or communing with nature."

"I see."

"I do not believe you do. I can tell by your tone of voice that you think her selfish."

"I did not suggest that she was selfish. You did, Eric."

"She might have been, a little," he admitted reluctantly, then yawned.

"I think you must rest now."

"Do not go! I have rested quietly," he complained, "and for the greater part of seven days. Oh, God, what a damned fool I was," he said with a groan. "But who would have reckoned on the wind? Julia, you do not think I will go blind, do you?"

"My dear, the doctor has said there is no chance of that."

"How can he be sure?" He moved restlessly. "Oh, God, if I should be blind . . ."

"Mr. Chatterton is not unfamiliar with your condition, Eric, my dear. He has told Laura that he treated a man with a similar disorder last year. He said that the patient was in considerably worse straits than yourself—having been even closer to the flames. The canopy of his bed was burning."

"Really? I wonder why Laura did not tell me about that."

"She told me. I expect she thought I would pass it on to you."

"She has come to depend on you for many things, has she not, Julia?"

"There is much she must do, Eric. I try to help her. . . ."

"And does administering to her useless husband come

under the heading 'helping Laura'?"

"You know that is not why I come, Eric."

"Do I?"

"Yes. And now I really must go."

"I have made you angry." He sighed.

"No, but I must go. I have been with you for quite a while."

"And now you are tired and bored."

"You know that I am not," she said, chidingly.

"When will you return?" he asked eagerly.

"Tomorrow."

"Why not tonight?"

"Laura has told me that she will be with you tonight. We must consider Laura, Eric."

"Oh, God, I know." He groaned. He added a trifle resentfully, "You did not worry about your sister's feelings quite so much last week."

"The circumstances were hardly the same last week, Eric."

"That is true . . . and do you know, Julia, you have changed in other ways?"

"Have I? I am not aware of it."

"Last week I thought you were somewhat lacking in kindness, Julia."

"Did you?" A little gurgle of laughter escaped her. "I thought I was being very kind to you, Eric."

He laughed. "You were wickedly provocative, my dear, and as I think I have told you, I did not like your jibes at poor Laura."

"You keep referring to those. How often must I tender my abject apologies, even though you, my dear, were not so kind, either."

"I never criticized my wife, but . . ." He sighed. "You are right. I wanted to be with you even when my conscience told me that I was wrong. Indeed, I am inclined to believe that I am reaping the rewards of sin."

"We did not sin, Eric."

"My strength was failing, and you, teasing me with your chancy touches and coming to me in the night with your tales of strange sounds."

"I heard strange sounds, Eric."

"Did you?"

"I thought I did . . . and the inn was reputed to be haunted. I meant nothing by it. I wanted only a little comfort in the night. And you gave it to me."

"And received small comfort from the gesture, I can tell you."

"I expect I should applaud your strength of character." She laughed mirthlessly.

"You should, since it was put to the extreme test."

"I will have to tell Laura how you resisted me."

"You will tell her nothing!" he said fiercely, half sitting up.

"Eric, dear, lie down." She gently pushed him back on his pillows.

"You will tell her nothing," he repeated.

"I was only teasing you. I begin to believe that you do care for Laura, after all."

"I do care for her. She is uncommonly kind and incredibly undemanding."

"Unlike myself, I expect?"

"Entirely unlike you, Julia, or so I must have said four days ago."

"You have changed your mind?"

"I do not know . . ." He paused at a tap on the door. "Are you being summoned?"

"I will see, and if you will remember, I did tell you that it was time for you to rest." She hurried to the door and opened it a crack. "Yes?" she said in a low voice.

"Milady, Lady Orville is below," the servant said in a low voice.

"Oh, dear . . . tell her that I will be down directly."

"Yes, milady."

She moved back to the bed. "I must leave you, Eric. Indeed, I should have left you at least an hour ago. I beg you will try to sleep now."

"Who wants you?" he demanded fretfully.

"Lady Orville is here. She is inquiring about your health."

"She is Laura's friend. Why cannot Laura see her?"

"Laura is not here. She is riding, as I think I explained earlier. Furthermore, we have been conversing far too long. You must rest."

"When will you return, Julia?"

"Later, I promise you." She bent to kiss him on the cheek, and then as he caught at her arm, she gently disengaged herself from his weakened hold and hurried out of the room, closing the door softly behind her.

She did not go down the stairs immediately. Instead, she leaned against the wall, steeling herself for the ordeal of meeting her friend. She had been extremely relieved that Lady Orville had not come to visit her during the first and most crucial week of Eric's illness. She might have been moved to tell her of the madness that had been taking place within the confines of his room, and she would have been in no mood to hear Millicent's remarks on her folly. In fact, she was still unwilling to engage in what she feared must be a verbal fencing match. Probably she would have been far wiser to have told her abigail that she was resting. Still, given Lady Orville's almost supernatural perspicacity, she was quite sure that such an excuse would have been regarded as an excuse, and furthermore, a part of her did want to see the lady. She enjoyed their friendship, and she had always found her frankness refreshing. However, on this occasion she was resolved to steel herself against making revelations she would regret later—given the latter's sharp tongue and freely expressed opinions.

She went to her chamber and looked in the mirror. As she had anticipated, her hair was in need of combing. She did not ring for her abigail, she did not wish to meet Lucy's commiserating gaze in the mirror, and to be aware of words unsaid quivering between them. As usual, she was conscious of surprise as she stared at her mirrored countenance. In less than a week it was much thinner. Her cheekbones were more prominent, her eyes seemed larger, and her chin appeared more pointed with its slight cleft deepened. She had lost weight—a surprising amount, she suspected, for her gowns were looser.

The process had already been underway before Eric's accident and augmented by her worry and by her loss of appetite. However, she had no time to dwell on these changes now. She ran a comb through her hair and was, as always, grateful that it curled naturally. Then she went down to meet Lady Orville.

"My dear," her friend remarked as Laura hurried into the drawing room. "I vow, you must have lost a stone!"

"I expect I have lost some weight, Millicent. It is good to see you."

"It is good to see you, too, my dear. You are looking very pretty, and how am I to address you? Am I to call you Laura or Julia?"

Laura tensed. "I . . . I am not sure I understand you," she said, faltering.

"I am sorry, my dear. I expect my first question should have concerned Eric, but I am given to understand that he is as well as can be expected given his accident. I acquired this information from the same source who was kind enough to provide me with some details concerning your—er, masquerade."

"Who—" Laura began angrily.

Lady Orville held up her hand. "My love, I obtained the information through the usual sources, and did I not tell you that you cannot keep secrets from the servants? There is always a leak, no matter how careful you believe you have been."

"Oh, God." Laura ran a nervous hand through her hair. "If Eric should learn . . ."

"Eric will not learn anything, my dear. He will remain in undeserved bliss until Julia takes it into what passes for her mind to depart for Cornwall. In my estimation she never should have come, and certainly her continued presence here is causing confusion, concern, and controversy."

"Oh, God." Laura groaned. "How many know?"

"You can comfort yourself with the fact that a great many may know whom you do not know and will never meet. However, if I have heard it, you may be assured that there might be some uncommon gossip in other quarters. I expect, my dear, that it will blow away before Eric rises from his bed of pain."

"He must not be told!" Laura said fiercely. "Rather I would dismiss the whole staff, or better yet, take him to some seaside resort where we are not known."

"Oh, Laura, Laura, Laura, my poor child . . . why are you so determined to let him remain in this state of confusion?" Lady Orville demanded.

Laura regarded her angrily, and at the same time concernedly. "Could I have let him know that Julia left at five in the morning following his accident? They . . . they had become very close friends, you know. It was my fault that she went. I drove her away."

"I am informed that it was I who drove her away," Lady Orville said crisply.

"You?"

"That is what my Nancy told me."

"If Lucy . . ." Laura began with a frown.

"Do not even think of Lucy, my dear Laura. Your abigail is known to be 'horridly closemouthed,' according to Nancy—at least when it comes to your impersonation. However, you cannot depend on the same staunch loyalty from servants you hardly know, and so I know that your staff has been adjured on pain of death not to reveal that Lady Ludlow dashed out of here as soon as she might."

"Oh, dear." Laura groaned. "Our servants were never so loquacious at home."

"I am positive that that cannot be true." Lady Orville smiled. "You, from your own account, were far too immersed in your books to pay heed to idle gossip. I, on the other hand, have always been fascinated by it. Consequently, each morning when Nancy fixes my hair, I have a lively account of all that has been taking place in the houses of my friends and, I must admit, my enemies. Who was it first had the information that Lady Cawood ran away with her groom? And who was it who first learned about young Ned Bannister's being forced to wed his sister's governess, which he did under duress and only a month before their son was born? Unfortunately the governess turned out to be of noble birth—else she could have been pensioned off. I understand, however, that they are quite happy and have added two more chicks to their nest. Certainly I have always enjoyed this early information. But I must needs make an exception in your case, Laura, my love. I find this particular tale both fascinating and depressing. Is it not time that your ailing lord became better acquainted with the woman he married, rather than with the female he did not marry, and were he aware of her character, or rather the lack of it, he would not have looked at twice?"

"You do not understand," Laura said unhappily.

"Oh, yes, and are you aware that you are doing him an extreme disservice in denying him your real self? In his weakened state he will convince himself that he is deeply in love with Julia, and when he realizes that she has gone, which will happen immediately he is on his feet again, how do you think he will feel?

"I do not, mind you, hold any briefs for him. He will deserve his disappointment, every ounce of it, but certainly you will not be any the happier for it. Do you intend to spend your life in this state of confusion?"

Laura was silent for a moment. Then she said reluctantly, "I think you are right."

"Then if you believe I am right, I suggest you rectify this wrong as soon as possible."

"I . . . I think I should wait until he is a little less anxious over his condition," Laura said.

"And meanwhile you will continue to enact the role of charming Julia?"

"A very little longer," Laura said pleadingly.

Lady Orville sighed and shook her head. "Laura, do you know, when I was sixteen, my father took myself, my sister, and my brother on the Grand Tour? We saw many fascinating sights, but the one that intrigued me the most was the Colosseum in Rome, where they used to hold the games. We, my father and I, climbed up the steps of the arena and inscribed our names at the top, where there were already many other names. Then we sat down and imagined what it must have been like when the ancient Romans sat there to view the Christians being devoured by lions. Our guide told us that they went to their fates quite happily—secure that in suffering for their beliefs they would gain a seat in heaven. And you, suffering for your love, must be equally sure of a heavenly perch—else you would send Julia on her way with a well-aimed brick to her phantom head."

"How lovely to see the Roman Colosseum." Laura murmured.

"That was not the point of my story," Lady Orville said with pardonable exasperation.

"I will tell him that I must go . . . or rather that she must go . . . soon."

"Tomorrow," Lady Orville said firmly.

"Well, perhaps." Laura sighed. "He is so unhappy and so frightened, though you would never know it from either his speech or his manner."

"But you know it," Lady Orville said.

"How could I not?"

"And how could he not know that you are playing a trick on him—a rather despicable trick?"

"A . . . a despicable trick?" Laura questioned angrily.

"Are you being fair to him? Are you not heaping coals of fire on your own head for your so-called absences from his side?"

"He does not appear to miss me." Laura said dryly.

"How can he miss you when he is constantly confronted by your adulterous sister? No doubt, though he would not say so to *her,* he feels himself sadly neglected by you."

"I come to him in my own person, and he never even inquires as to my whereabouts when I am not with him."

"I'll wager he thinks you have been in the library. I cannot imagine that he fears the rivalry of a book or, indeed, your little librarian, nice lad that he is."

"He is very intelligent," Laura said. "And he has found so many wonderful volumes—"

"Do not get me off the subject. Do not wait another day, Laura. Tell your lord that the beautiful Julia has departed for Cornwall."

"I think I will wait just another day," Laura said stubbornly.

"And tomorrow you will leave? Or, rather, she will leave?"

"Yes." Laura sighed. "I expect she must."

"And that is a promise?" Lady Orville caught and held Laura's eyes with a probing stare.

"I have told you that I would," Laura said impatiently.

"If it is not a promise, my love, I will find a way to betray you."

"You would not!" Laura cried.

"If it is a promise, as you have said, I will not need to betray you—but rest assured, my dear, I will know one way or the other," Lady Orville said solemnly. "And now, since I have the feeling that you are much in need of a nap, I will leave you."

"Must you go so quickly?" Laura protested.

"Yes, my dear, because you do look frazzled. I do wish you were of an opinion which is not only mine but that of all those who have met you. . . . Eric is indeed fortunate to have so caring and so lovely a bride. And if he does not realize that earlier rather than later, it is entirely your own fault!"

Laura, seeing her guest to the door, waved as Lady Orville walked away, disappearing around a bend in the road. She was sorry to see her go, and then, conversely, she was not. She needed to think. The situation in which she now found herself was peculiarly daunting, especially since it was no longer confined to the house but known and, through the medium of gossiping servants, spread far beyond these walls.

If it were to reach Eric's ears, what would he think? He would be angry and embarrassed, certainly. Furthermore, it would be difficult for her to explain why she had done it. . . . No, she thought unhappily, he would not need that particular explanation. He would know why and with that knowledge would come that which she wished to spare him—guilt. Yet it was unlikely that enlightenment would reach him here in this household, and meanwhile, were she to cease her impersonation and tell him that Julia had been called away, would he not regret her passing? And would she not regret it even more?

With a little shock she realized that yes, yes, yes, she would certainly regret "Julia's" departure. When she had initially indulged in this pretense, it had been difficult, but it had grown easier and easier, and indeed, she had actually seemed to be Julia, lovely, beguiling Julia. She had found it remarkably easy to flirt with Eric, to cajole and tease him, something that was beyond the capacity of Laura—and why was that? She had no answers . . . she could only cite a certain freedom that came with the pretense, as if, indeed, she were a butterfly emerging from a confining cocoon to realize that those flat things bound at her sides were, in effect, wings to bear her up toward the sun!

"One more night," she murmured, resenting Millicent as she never had before, the while regretfully acknowledging to herself that she was right. However, she was Laura at this moment, and as Laura, she must get another book from the library. She had been reading Donne, but he had mentioned liking the works of Coleridge, and perhaps she would read him *The Rime of the Ancient Mariner* or *Christabel* or even *Kubla Khan.*

As she came into the library she found, as always, Mr. Quinn at his desk, happily surrounded by stacks of books. As she entered, he looked up quickly and smiled shyly.

"Good afternoon, Lady Marne," he said respectfully.

"Good afternoon, Mr. Quinn," Laura responded. "I came to see if we had any of Coleridge's works, and also to hope that you have made some new discoveries."

His eyes glinted with pleasure and enthusiasm. "Oh, I have, your ladyship, the most exciting discoveries, two volumes written by the Abbe Michel de Marolles, who lived in France in the seventeenth century, His *Quatrains sur la Personnes de la Cour et les Gens de Lettres.* This is exceedingly rare. I can only imagine that one of his lordship's ancestors must have found it during a visit to France in the 1600s."

"Oh," Laura breathed, "that is exciting!"

"Furthermore, it is in exceedingly good condition—rather, they are. There are several volumes." He indicated a table where a number of small leather-bound books were spread. "Also, I have found an old *Heptaemeron* of the Queen of Navarre."

"Oh, yes, that is a collection of tales not unlike the *Decameron,* is it not?"

He nodded. "However, it is considerably less salacious."

"I know." She gave him a mischievous smile. "I rather enjoyed parts of the *Decameron,* though. We had one in our library at home, and I used to spend a great deal of time there."

"Really?"

She nodded, wondering why he looked surprised. "Yes, when I was not riding, it was my favorite place to be. I used to wish that I might write as well."

"I imagine you could were you to try," he said shyly.

"I have tried. I did not expect to be married, you see." She reddened. "I expect I should not have told you that."

He appeared even more surprised. "But now that you have, milady, why would you not expect it? I hope you do not find my question impertinent?"

"Oh, no, of course I do not," she assured him hastily. "It is only that my mother, my grandmother, too, did not believe I would be—being the youngest and less favored of three sisters. Until I met my husband I was forever in libraries or, as I have told you, riding, and when we came to London, I would ride in the park and visit the British Museum."

"I wish I might have known you then," he said quickly, and blushed. "I hope you will not believe me impertinent, but I have never met a female so knowledgeable about books."

"I love them, and as I have already told you, I do not believe you impertinent. I wish we had met, sir. I did not like London when I first came. Furthermore, I thought it was very silly coming there on the strength of a prediction!"

"A prediction?" he questioned in surprise.

Laura laughed and rolled her eyes, "My grandmother's abigail—Jane, her name is—predicted that I would be married, and since she has always been quite amazingly accurate in her prognostications, it was decided by my grandmother and my mother that I must be presented at Court and have a season in London."

"And lo, the seeress proved to be right." He smiled. "Though if you will excuse the liberty, milady, I cannot imagine that prediction or no prediction, you would have gone in want of a husband."

"Do you not?" Laura regarded him in a surprise equal to his own. "My sisters, my brother, and my mama, also my grandmother, were convinced that I would be a prop to Mama, or something like. I do not imagine that I was precisely meant to be a prop, since I was always, as I told you, reading or riding and never where Mama wanted me on the few times she needed me." Laura blushed. "Gracious, I fear I am talking far too much and interrupting your work, Mr. Quinn."

"Oh, no, never," he protested vehemently. "I do find your interruptions delightful, though again I do think you refine too much upon your previous fears. I cannot imagine that your mother ever could have expected *you* to be a prop to her."

"Well, actually, she did eventually discard the idea. She used to fulminate greatly upon my unsuitability for the position. She was planning to recruit one of my widowed cousins were she ever to require such aid."

He regarded her with ever-increasing surprise. "Do

you know, Lady Marne, I believe you to be perfectly serious."

"Of course I am," she responded. "Why would I not be? It is no more than the truth, and I have no doubt but that I must have been a wretched companion."

"I do not understand such thinking, milady."

"And I am beginning not to understand you." Laura smiled. "But enough, I thought that if my husband is restive in the night, I had better find something soothing to read to him—I was thinking about Coleridge's poems."

"Coleridge is very well, but if you will forgive the liberty, Wordsworth might be more soothing, and I have just discovered a fine edition of his poems."

"Oh, have you? Eric might enjoy Wordsworth's nature poems. His wife was particularly fond of flowers and other growing things. I trust you have seen the conservatory?"

"His . . . wife?" the librarian asked confusedly.

"Lady Christina, his first wife," Laura amended with a blush. "I expect you have not visited the conservatory, but you may if you choose."

"I should like to see it, certainly, but I am more partial to flowers growing out-of-doors and wildly rather than confined to narrow beds in a garden—though those I have seen here are very beautiful."

"I think I might agree with you," Laura said. "I have always enjoyed the woods myself, but so did she, Lady Christina, poor girl."

"She must have died young," he commented.

"She was very young," Laura nodded. "He misses her dreadfully."

"He misses her now, milady?"

Laura flushed, suddenly and uncomfortably aware that she was being far too frank and confidential with a veritable stranger, even though Mr. Quinn did not seem to be a stranger. In fact, she realized with a slight shock, she was well on the way to thinking of him as a good friend rather than a paid employee come to catalogue the

library. However, it was far too late to withdraw coldly
into the guise of the unapproachable peeress she was
supposed to be. She said, "They were very happy, I
understand. She was his first love." Another confidence
trembled on her tongue and was ruthlessly swallowed.
Yet the words echoing through her mind were loud in
that unspoken affirmation: *And my sister Julia is his
second.*

"Has she been gone long?" he asked.

Less than a week. Fortunately Laura was able to
swallow those words too. "She died two years ago," she
responded.

"I see," he said thoughtfully. He looked as if he would
have liked to comment further on the subject of her late
ladyship, but instead he said, "I will fetch the Wordsworth, and there is also a Coleridge—if you decide to
read from it."

"No, I believe you are right. I rather think my husband
would prefer Wordsworth. I do thank you, Mr. Quinn."

"I am delighted that I have been able to help you,
milady."

As Laura emerged from the library she saw the housekeeper hurrying down the hall. The woman was looking
harried, she thought anxiously. "Is . . . is there anything
the matter, Mrs. Wilson?" she asked.

The latter came to a startled stop. "Oh, milady, I was
looking for you. His lordship is wanting you."

"Oh, dear." Laura gave her an anxious look. "I
thought he was asleep."

"No, milady," Mrs. Wilson said. She added meaning-
fully, "And he wants *you.*"

"He wants Laura?" Laura asked, feeling oddly de-
tached from herself as if, she, as Julia, was wondering
why he would be asking for her tiresome sister.

"Yes, milady," the housekeeper affirmed with a slight
grimace.

"I am sure you and the staff must find this extremely
confusing," Laura said regretfully.

"Oh, no, milady, I do understand. It were that hard for

him when poor Lady Christina died. And your sister bein' so like her. If . . . if you will forgive the liberty, it must be hard for you now. You must feel as if you weren't married at all."

Laura sighed. "I am not sure how I feel, Mrs. Wilson. My only real interest lies in keeping my husband happy."

The housekeeper smiled. "You are uncommonly kind, milady." Bobbing a curtsy, she hurried back the way she had come.

Laura looked after her and was immediately regretful that she had not said something to her about the unfortunate leakage Lady Orville had brought to her attention, but what might she have said? It was late to say anything. However, it was time that Julia returned to Cornwall, certainly. Julia to Cornwall and Christina to her grave, since it was quite possible that Julia was only a surrogate for Christina.

" 'Oh, what a tangled web we weave, when first we practice to deceive!' " Laura thought unhappily, and then remembered that the quotation was from Scott, and perhaps Eric would like Julia to read from Marmion on this last night. But, she decided, Wordsworth would be more calming than Scott's warlike images.

"Is it you, then, Laura?" the man on the bed asked, as Laura closed the door behind her.

"Yes, Eric," she replied in slightly harder tones than those she employed as Julia. "My sister is resting now. You wanted me?"

"Yes, Laura. I have not . . . seen much of you lately. Or rather, you have not come to visit me. Where have you been keeping yourself?"

There was an aggrieved note in his voice, almost as if he had been missing *her,* a sentiment he did not share with her sister, certainly. She said, "Oh, I have ridden and I have read. Mr. Quinn has found some very interesting and valuable volumes."

"So I have been given to understand. You spend a great deal of time in the library, do you not, Laura?"

"Yes, as you know, I love to read."

"And has the industrious Mr. Quinn found you much in the way of reading matter?"

"A great deal. When you are better, Eric, dear, I am sure you will be amazed and delighted by his discoveries."

"What does he do with his time when he is not in the library?"

"I do not know," Laura said. "He spends a great many hours there, though. He has told me that his work here is as exciting to him as say gambling is to those who enjoy it."

"Indeed? I would think the work is not dissimilar. For every fine volume he finds, there must be many others that are not worth his ferreting them out."

"He has not told me about those," Laura said. "He does say that he does not imagine that it has been catalogued in quite some time."

"That is entirely true." Eric sighed. "I blame myself for neglecting the library and, indeed, the greater part of the house. I am sure there is much to be done in many rooms—repainting, refinishing. In the days before we married, I had the workmen I employed concentrate mainly on the suite we would share." He sighed. "And now I am bound here like a prisoner with an indefinite sentence."

"Come," she said cajolingly, "it is not quite that bad. The doctor has assured me—"

"The doctor, the doctor . . ." he said, interrupting impatiently and a trace angrily. "How can I trust him? He will tell me what I wish to hear rather than what he believes to be true!"

"No, Eric, you are wrong. I have spoken to him, and he has explained that rest is needed . . . both for your eyes and for your ankle and leg."

A long sigh escaped him. He reached up a hand and touched the bandage around his eyes. "No more than a week has passed, and I am already weary of the darkness," he said fretfully. "And I am sure I weary others as well with my complaints. You and your sister have been uncommonly kind, but it cannot be pleasant for Julia . . . for either of you . . . to sit here in this darkened chamber reading to an invalid."

"You are a temporary invalid, Eric. And neither Julia nor myself has complained."

"Laura, I am worried about Julia." He frowned.

"Worried?" she repeated in some surprise. "Why?"

"She has been here for quite a while and her husband must wonder why. . . ."

"But she is at odds with her husband," Laura reminded him.

"I cannot understand that," he murmured. "He must be a damned fool."

"I think he is passing fond of her."

"Then he is doubly damned. Oh, God, I am sorry, Laura. I do not know what I am saying. This damnable darkness has clouded my wits."

"I think you must rest," Laura said gently.

"Must I rest? Must I, indeed?" he asked mockingly. "I have been doing nothing else, my dear Laura."

"And that is as it should be."

"Of course, you are right, Laura, my dear, sensible Laura. Have I ever told you that I believe you imbued with all the virtues?"

She tensed slightly and managed a little laugh. "If you have, I do not remember it, and if you believe that I am so imbued, I will tell you that you are mistaken."

"Ah, no, I am not," he said. "It is amazing. . . ."

"Amazing?" she questioned.

"You . . . you have so very little in common with your sister."

Laura tensed but managed to say easily, "I am quite aware of that, Eric."

He moved restlessly. "If you imagine that I am complimenting Julia, I am not. Indeed, it were better . . ." He paused, frowning.

"I do not understand you," Laura finally said after a lapse of two or three minutes during which time he appeared to be groping for words.

"Give me your hand, Laura."

Laura reached out to grasp Eric's hand gently, and in a moment he had lifted his other hand to imprison it. "I am fond of you, Laura, dear. I . . . I do not want you to believe that because . . . in the past I have seemed aloof and distracted, that I have meant to be uncaring of your feelings. I do care, and I do appreciate your great kindness. You are patience itself. Oh, Lord, it is warm in here!" He dropped her hand and moved restlessly on his pillows.

Laura put her hand on his forehead. "I do hope you are not running a fever," she said anxiously.

"If frustration and impatience be a sort of fever, I am afflicted with two fevers." He groaned.

"All things come to an end," she said soothingly. "Your ordeal will be over sooner than you imagine, Eric, my dear."

"I would like to believe that." He paused, and then burst out, "Your sister Julia, Laura, she ought to go."

"Why? Does she not please you, Eric?"

"Of course she pleases me," he said irritably. "But it is not her place to be here, administering to me. It cannot be very pleasant for her."

"She has not complained."

"No, I am sure she would not. Still, she must have friends in London and elsewhere. I am sure she did not plan to remain here so long."

"Do you want me to tell her to go?" Laura asked.

"Yes . . . no, say nothing. I will tell her. I expect she will be here later. She usually comes in before she retires. But of course I am telling you nothing that you do not know."

"Has my sister angered you in any way, Eric?"

"No," he said hastily. "I feel, however, that she cannot be very happy here. She must believe herself between Scylla and Charybdis, leaving a jealous husband in Cornwall and coming here to weary herself at my bed-side."

"Julia is much distressed over your accident, Eric. She blames herself for it."

"And pities me accordingly?" he questioned bitterly. Before she could respond, he added, "It is not her fault, as I have told her, as I have told you—it is a tradition, the lighting of the midsummer fires. It has usually gone off safely enough."

"I fear the wind flouted tradition," Laura commented.

"Yes." He actually chuckled. "That sounds like something Julia might say. You do seem remarkably alike at times."

Laura tensed but said easily enough, "You are speaking of our voices, I expect. Mama used to be quite confounded by the similarity. She was actually pleased when Julia married and left the house."

"Was it an arranged marriage?" he asked.

"Oh, no," Laura assured him. "It was love at first sight. Fortunately there was nothing to stand in their way."

"I see."

"I do believe you should rest now, Eric. We have talked long enough. The doctor has warned me that you must not become overtired."

"Very well, my dear. I expect I am a bit weary."

"I do know, of course. I will tell Mrs. Wilson that you are not to be disturbed until suppertime."

"Please," he murmured gratefully.

Coming out of his chamber, she closed the door softly behind her and stood there a moment, leaning against the wall, deeply regretting the promised leave-taking of "Julia," for there would now be even more awkwardness between them because of her foolish and possibly wicked masquerade. He would miss Julia, and conversely—or perhaps perversely, as she had already decided—she would miss her too.

"One more night only," Laura whispered, and regretted the lift of the heart that the decision engendered.

In spite of that decision, Laura delayed her visit until nine that night, mainly because it would be near Eric's bedtime, and Julia's moments with him would be accordingly curtailed. She did not ask herself why she found this delay expedient—yet as she finally stood before his door again, she had a strange, confused feeling that she was really leaving, and the person remaining behind was no more than a wax image imbued with spurious life.

The reality was Julia, beloved Julia, who, like Caesar, came, saw, and conquered. "She" had annexed Eric so easily! She had only needed to lift a beckoning finger and match it with an equally beckoning smile. Those were the aids to the voice they both shared, but only on Julia's lips was it truly beguiling. Julia had been born beguiling, their mother had averred. She had been her father's favorite, the father Laura had never known. Would it have been different had he lived to see his last child? Might he not have been fond of her too? It was not easy to be a posthumous child . . . an unwanted third daughter, born to a grieving mother who had hoped for a second son.

Her thoughts must be banished before she turned the handle of Eric's door. They must needs remain beyond the threshold! This was Julia's hour, and he needed her tonight. He was restless, Mrs. Wilson had said, concern written large on her face.

"Tossin' 'n' turning he's been. . . . It seems he had a bad dream, milady. He's always had an active imagination. When he was a lad, it was hard for him to tell the difference between dreams and reality. Later he started writing little stories. His tutors said he had promise, but his father laughed at the idea."

"He should have encouraged him," Laura had said hotly.

"His father did not hold with him bein' bookish, milady."

"I hope that he will take it up again," Laura said.

"Perhaps he might if someone was to encourage him . . . ." The housekeeper's meaning had been clear.

She would encourage Eric, Laura thought, when he

was better. That she could do and was pleased that the library was finally taking shape. That might provide the incentive he needed. However, she could not think of that, either. This was Julia's last night, a time of farewells and, she thought with a little shiver, exorcism, for in essence, Julia was a specter, a specter in a great house that had no ghosts but many, many memories. Indeed, Julia herself was a memory, brought to spurious life by a trick of the voice.

She drew a long breath and released it. Then she opened the door and came inside. She closed the door quietly, but if he was awake, the man on the bed would hear the click of the latch. If he was not awake, she would leave quickly, as quietly as she had come—more quietly, even.

"Julia . . ." His muted voice seemed to caress her name. "Is that you?"

She hastened to the bed. "Yes . . . are you feeling better, my dear?"

"I am now." He made no effort to conceal his gladness.

"You have had a restless afternoon, I hear."

"Must you leave, Julia?" he demanded. Without giving her a chance to respond, he added, "But you must, I know."

"Yes, I must, for . . . my own peace of mind."

"And also for mine." He groaned. "Oh, Julia, Julia, we should have met either sooner or later."

"I know," she said softly. "It would have been best for both of us."

"Life is full of unkind tricks." He sighed. "Oh, God, I wish I could see you." He shuddered. "I had a dream, a dream of being lost in perpetual darkness." He shuddered. "Is there something I have not been told, Julia?"

"No, nothing," she assured him quickly, catching his hand and holding it gently. "The doctor has told Laura that your eyes will heal easily enough. It is not an uncommon accident, Eric, my dear."

He eased his hand from her grasp, then, with a lightning move, caught her hand and brought it to his lips. "What will I do without you, Julia?" he asked huskily and with an edge of desperation to his tone.

"There is Laura," she said softly. "There must be Laura, Eric."

"Yes." He groaned. "She is so good, so patient, so very unexciting."

"Yes." She sighed. "I know."

"And both of you born to the same parents."

"I was my father's favorite . . . Poor Laura had no father. She was not wanted. A son was wanted when she arrived and surprised us all. Mama was particularly disappointed."

"I gathered as much, poor girl. Is there a moon tonight, Julia?"

"A moon?" she repeated, startled by his change of subject.

"I seem to be seeing you in moonlight."

"Yes, there is a moon . . . a three-quarter moon, Eric."

"That is quite enough to gild your face . . . Julia by moonlight. Put my hand against your cheek, Julia."

She gently took his hand and guided it to her cheek, glad that the contours of her face had changed in the last week. They were much less plump than they had been, mainly because, as the housekeeper had accused, she had merely picked at her food. Then her thoughts were abruptly scattered as Eric put his arms around her and drew her against him.

"To touch you is to want you," he whispered. "But I will not, dare not, take you. I wish only that you lie by my side, my Julia."

She remembered what he had said earlier—had it been today or yesterday, she was not sure. Her thoughts were jumbled, scattered, but had he not accused her of leading him on? Now he was doing the leading, the persuading, and his fingers had trailed down her cheek to her shoulder, pushing down her loose shift, the shift she had worn on other occasions when she had come to comfort him in the night—when he had cried out in pain and in distress.

"Let me feel your warmth, Julia," he was saying, "and then go . . . go quickly, for both our sakes. You must not stay. Promise me that you will not stay."

"I should not," she murmured, "but . . ."

His laughter, low and unfamiliar, was in her ears. "Please," he murmured.

Her heart was beating in her throat. She must go, and hastily, hastily, but Eric's hand was on her arm; it was hard on her arm and there was a pulse that had escaped her throat and was beating . . . where? She was not sure. There were other pulses, many pulses coursing through her body, so that almost without volition she responded to his prompting and at length lay beside him without quite knowing how she had come to be there so quickly.

His lips were on her cheeks, her neck, and then at the pulsing hollow beneath her throat, and his hands caught at her shift, pushing it down. She did not know how or when she suddenly became aware that she was without it, lying close beside him, feeling the warm, pulsating length of his own nakedness against her and his passionate, invading kisses, forcing her lips apart, and she, in turn, pressing against him, thrilled by his excitement and on fire with her own excitement, and by feelings for which she had no name. Then she felt as though she were borne aloft by a passion that seemed to be taking her out of her body . . . the while he held her tightly, tightly, tightly, so tightly, that they were welded together in an ecstatic union that abolished self—making her one with the man who had possessed her.

Finally he released her. "Oh, God, oh, Julia," he said brokenly. "Oh, God, what can I say?"

"And I . . ." she meant to say, but at first no words would come. "And I," she managed to murmur finally, saying on a fractured breath, "I must go."

"Not yet." He groped for her and found her arm and clasped it. "Oh, Julia, Julia, I did not mean for this to happen, for all that I have wanted you. It . . . it was the thought of your leaving, but . . . oh, God, I could not have been thinking at all."

"Nor I." She sighed, loathing the role she had played, the perilous masquerade, which had ended as dangerously as it was fated to end, leaving her fulfilled yet unfulfilled, because of her husband's surging guilt and grief. "But," she could not help telling him, "it . . . was so beautiful."

"For me, too, Julia. . . . Oh, God, for me, too, but . . ." His hand was on her arm and slipped to cradle her breast and was taken away hastily. "Go, my very dearest, please go, else I shall not have the strength to let you go."

"Yes, yes, of course, my dearest," she breathed. "I . . . I am sorry."

"The fault was mine." He groaned. "All mine . . . oh, God, Julia, if only you had remained as before."

"As . . . before?" she murmured confusedly.

"Teasing me, driving me to distraction . . . but not to your bed, my love. You made me angry, then . . . but tonight you were different, so different . . . another Julia entirely, and one I . . . I could not resist."

"Forgive me," she whispered.

"Oh, God, that is not for you to say, my angel, but for me. . . . Forgive me, but go, please go."

"Yes, of course, my very dearest." She sighed and reluctantly slid from his side, shivering as she felt the chilly floor against her bare feet and the evening breeze enveloping her nakedness.

She groped for her shift and, finding it, hastily donned it. Then, without another word, she hurried to the door and came into the hall, closing the door softly behind her.

In another few minutes she was in her own bed wishing . . . but it was no time for wishing. It was a time for praying that no more explanations would be needed, praying that Julia's promised departure on the morrow would help assuage her husband's guilt and her own.

EIGHT

AND WHY ARE YOU NOT RIDING?" Lady Orville demanded.

"I am sorry, Millicent. Did you not get my note?" Laura asked.

"I did, and since it is the third in a week, I, as your good friend and concerned over your well-being, wish to know why." She bent a probing eye on Laura's face. "You are pale, even paler than Wednesday week, and you are certainly thinner. I will not call it unbecoming, but still, it is not healthy. If you are not careful, you will waste away to a mere wraith, and in time Eric will have to contend with another ghost."

"Oh"—Laura forced a laugh—"you do talk such nonsense, Millicent."

Lady Orville looked around the drawing room. "The draperies are gone. I am glad you are making these changes. I much prefer the blue. I always thought there was far too much green, and I really loathe the colors Eric's mother chose too. They were very trying, even to one as fair as the late Christina . . . what a pleasure to speak about her as having been rather than still here."

"Do you consider that quite kind?" Laura inquired.

"Of course I do not. One ought to speak well of the dead, if possible. It is that 'if possible' that gives me leeway when it comes to Christina. Your eyes are enormous, Laura. You have high cheekbones too. Have you given up eating?"

Laura stifled a sigh. In the last fortnight she had been purposely avoiding her dear friend because she feared her probing glances and her frank speech. She said carefully, "I have not been feeling quite myself of late. I expect that my concern over Eric has told on me a bit."

"I do not know why it should have," Lady Orville said blandly. "The fact that you have spent hours and hours in his chamber, watching over him . . . that you have seen no one and have done nothing save fret over his condition, the while you have been making light of it to him and assuaging his fears of possible blindness, not to mention soaking his ankle and massaging his leg . . . none of these minor duties can have had a deleterious effect on your state of health." She shook her head, adding ruefully, "Oh, my dear, dear Laura, I very much fear that you are the stuff of which martyrs are made!" She frowned and scanned Laura's face. "You do look peaked. I would have imagined that since the fortuitous departure of your . . . sister, you would be far less overwrought and feeling much more the thing. Yet to my mind you seem even less . . ." She paused as Laura suddenly coughed and, putting a hand to her chest, swallowed convulsively.

"I beg your pardon, Millicent," she said hastily. "I . . . had something indigestible for b-breakfast this morning and . . . and if you would excuse me for a moment, I will be back."

Without waiting for Lady Orville's response, Laura rushed out of the drawing room and, dashing up the stairs, reached her own chamber in time to make use of the bowl in the bathroom, an amenity installed by the late Lord Marne and particularly welcome at this time. A short time later, having washed her face, she stared at her image in the mirror and blinked away the tears she had not wanted her friend to see. A long sigh shook her. "Oh, why did she have to come here today?" she murmured unhappily.

"Because," said a tart voice from the doorway, "while she herself did not experience these symptoms until considerably later, servants talk, and she has had her ear to the ground as she understands savages do. Consequently she has heard the servants gossiping. My dearest Laura, nothing can be kept from the servants. I have sometimes believed that they have a set of signals superior to anything used on battlefields and might, indeed, be used to help England win her wars.

"Enough of nonsense, my love. Would I be wrong in imagining that Julia overplayed her hand or, rather, her role? I suspect that since he is none the wiser, Laura's habit of riding astride has had its effect on certain areas of her form, and that her maidenhead was ruptured by the saddle rather than by more felicitous exercises. You did tell me that you rode astride at home, did you not, Laura? Yes, you did, and were I a Bow Street Runner, my salary would be increased for this assumption, though I suspect you will be calling it 'presumption.' Do not be angry with me, my dearest Laura, but tell me, child, how long have you known?"

Laura regarded her, openmouthed. "How . . . how many people know? Has the tale spread far and wide?"

"No, my dearest, I have adjured my people to be as quiet as clams . . . if clams are really that quiet. They must communicate, must they not? Only we cannot hear them. Enough. The tale has not spread. And of course you have not said anything to Eric?"

"How can I say anything?" Laura asked miserably. "I beg you will keep this to yourself and t-tell your servants . . . but you have already done so."

"I have already done so," Lady Orville corroborated. "And I do not believe that anyone is going to penetrate the fastness of your . . . er, fortress and send up flares. Certainly I will not. You may trust me, you know."

"Oh, I . . . I do," Laura suddenly wailed. "Oh, M-Millicent, what am I to do? The doctor will be here two days hence to remove Eric's bandages from his eyes, and if I . . . should have a . . . a spell, what can I tell him?"

"My love." Lady Orville moved to Laura's side and put an arm around her shaking shoulders. "You will naturally tell him the truth."

"How can I?" Laura sobbed. "He would have to know the whole of it . . . everything. He will be angry and embarrassed, and ultimately he must be furious."

"He might very well be all of those things, my dear, but when he starts thinking about it and realizes the extent of your selflessness, your great kindness, I see a far different outcome than anything you might currently be envisioning. To my thinking, he will only love you the more."

"He . . . he will only l-love me the more?" Laura quavered. "But M-Millicent, he does not love me at all! And . . . and ever since that . . . that night . . ."

"The night before Julia's supposed departure? Yes, my dear Laura, I did hear about that from my abigail."

"They know . . . they know everything." Laura gasped in horror.

"No, my love, they might suspect, but they do not know. What is known is that Eric suddenly ceased to call upon Julia. It is also known that he told his valet that he was glad she had gone. He wished to be reassured, in fact, that she had actually departed."

"And . . . and what did his v-valet say?"

"He said that she was actually away, my love. I might add that he is very fond of you. I speak of Tim, the valet. He says that Lady Christina's not a patch on you . . . I have that from my abigail."

"Oh, dear, it is all so complicated—everything." Laura groaned. "And then there is Eric's vision. I pray that he will see . . . but what can he *think?*"

"You will tell him what he may think," Lady Orville said firmly. "And, my dear, do not worry. You will not have to blurt out the news directly the bandages are removed. As you are aware, I have a son and a daughter, aged respectively two and four, whom I rarely, if ever, mention mainly because they are not particularly interesting at these ages—at least not to outsiders. However, I can tell you that from these two past experiences, you will not begin to show for at least another two months, and fortunately the cut of our garments is not designed to reveal our conditions, as I think proved particularly convenient for Lady Hamilton some time back. And as for Eric's vision—of course he will see."

"Of course he will see, Lady Marne," the doctor, unconsciously, echoing Lady Orville's prognostications of a week earlier, smiled into Laura's anxious face. "If I could tell you the number of people I have treated for this condition—and some far worse off than your husband—you would be amazed and also heartened. Furthermore, his leg is healing well, and his ankle too. He is a strong, healthy young man. I have had the care of him for ten years, and he has lived a remarkably abstemious life for one in his social position. He is fond of the outdoors, he has always taken long walks, and he enjoys bowling, archery, and the like, which, I need not tell you, has given him the fine constitution he now possesses."

Laura nodded. "I know . . . but . . ."

"Let us not borrow trouble, milady," the doctor advised, and then gave her a long, measuring look. "You are looking rather pale, yourself, milady."

"I have not been feeling quite myself lately," Laura murmured, and swallowed a rising air bubble. "It is the anxiety, I expect," she added as another air bubble rose and was convulsively swallowed. She wished that the doctor's visit had not taken place on a morning when she had been feeling even worse than when she had discussed her condition with Lady Orville three days earlier. At present she was conscious of Mr. Chatterton's peculiarly penetrating stare. She felt a strong need to confide in him, but that was impossible, at least at present. Eric must be informed first, and how was she to manage that? It would mean revealing everything, and who would have thought that during her very first encounter with her husband . . . but she dared not think about that now, not when Mr. Chatterton was about to remove the bandages Eric had worn so long—actually it was not that long, a little over a month, but it had seemed aeons.

Standing at the end of the bed, Laura watched anxiously as Mr. Chatterton snipped through the cloth. Eric, himself, had fallen silent after greeting the doctor cordially, but with a strain in his voice that gave the lie to the smile that so valiantly curled his lips. "There, my lord." Mr. Chatterton put the bandages down on the table near Eric's bed.

"But . . . but it is still dark," Eric said shakily.

"Perhaps, my lord, it would not be so dark were you to open your eyes," the doctor said gently.

"Oh." Eric assayed a light laugh, which died a-borning as he opened his eyes and then said brokenly, "Oh, thank God, I can see!"

"Oh," Laura said, and then the chamber appeared to darken, and with a little moan she had a sense of falling and then knew no more.

Feeling most unwell, and with the strong smell of something burning close to her nostrils, Laura opened her eyes. She found herself lying on a chaise longue in her own chamber. Mr. Chatterton, bending over her, was removing a burnt feather from the immediate vicinity of her nose. She regarded him confusedly. "I . . . could not have . . . have swooned," she whispered.

"You did, my dear," the physician corroborated.

"I . . . I do not understand it." Laura convulsively swallowed more rising air bubbles. "I . . . I have never fainted before. I expect it is because I have been so anxious."

"Possibly, my dear young lady." The doctor nodded. "However, swoons can arise from a number of causes."

"C-could it have been s-something I may have eaten? I find that sometimes in the mornings—" She caught herself up. "I mean, at . . . at other times, too, I feel a little ill."

"Do you mean nauseated?" the doctor inquired.

"S-sometimes, but . . . but not always, and not always in the morning."

"I see." Mr. Chatterton smiled. "Now you had best lie still while I examine your husband's other injuries."

"But . . . but I am feeling much better," Laura protested, sitting up hastily, and then, regretfully, seeing the room seemingly swimming around her. "Oh, dear, I expect I am not . . . at least not yet."

"Please lie down, your ladyship," the doctor said crisply. "I will be back shortly."

Since the room was still exhibiting a strong tendency to whirl around her, Laura reluctantly lay back and closed her eyes as Mr. Chatterton hurried out.

"How is my wife?" Eric demanded anxiously as the doctor returned.

"She is resting—a slight upset," Mr. Chatterton said.

"She must have eaten something that disagreed with her," Eric said.

"Oh, I would not think so," the doctor murmured.

"Then what is the matter with her? She has been under a strain, I know. She has spent a great deal of time in here, and I know she has been anxious, though, bless her, she has never been anything but cheerful and confident that I would recover my sight."

"She is a most remarkable young woman," Mr. Chatterton agreed. "Unfortunately I do not believe she has taken the proper care of herself given her condition."

"Her condition?" Eric repeated. "She is not well?"

"Oh, I would imagine that she is well enough," the doctor assured him. "However, she has been most anxious, and at this time in her life she requires more rest." He smiled at Eric. "It is well that she has been reassured as to your eyesight. At least that will ease her mind. Your leg is on the mend, too, and while your ankle is still swollen, that, too, is a condition that will soon be alleviated. I should imagine that in another month and a half you should be as good as new. And by the time the child is born . . ."

"The . . . the child," Eric said faintly. "What . . . what may you mean, pray?"

Mr. Chatterton said genially, "I am sure that this will come as a surprise to you, my lord, but certainly it must be a welcome surprise. Your wife is expecting a child. I guessed that almost immediately. All the signs are there."

"A . . . a child," Eric regarded him in stunned amazement. "H-how c-could that . . . that be p-possible?"

It was the doctor's turn to be amazed. Then he smiled. "I expect she has not told you. I do not imagine that from all she has said that she is yet aware of her condition."

"I see," Eric said. "And . . . that is why she swooned?"

Mr. Chatterton nodded. "Yes, as I have said, she has been under a great strain. There have been times when I have been quite concerned about her. She is certainly devoted to you, my lord. But enough—I think I must tend her now . . . she will need certain instructions. And as I said, she needs to be made aware of her condition."

"Yes, indeed, she must," Eric said slowly. "You must apprise her of it immediately, I think."

"I will, of course. If you will excuse me, my lord?"

"A . . . a child," said Laura, staring at Mr. Chatterton confusedly. "You . . . did you t-tell Eric?"

Mr. Chatterton gave her a long, thoughtful look. "I did," he said, less warmly now. "Is there any reason why I should not have told him, milady?"

Meeting eyes which had turned from warmly amused to coldly suspicious, an unhappy Laura shook her head, saying faintly, "It is . . . only that I would rather have . . . have told him m-myself."

"I see." Mr. Chatterton's tone remained chilly. He said, "You must follow the directions I gave you, and I should like to see you again in two weeks, milady."

"You did not give me any directions, Mr. Chatterton," Laura said diffidently.

He frowned. "Oh, did I not? I suggest that you drink at least two glasses of milk per day, and I would advise you not to go riding. It is best that you have as much rest as possible. I will bid you good day, Lady Marne."

"Good day, Mr. Chatterton," Laura said faintly, pained by the change in his attitude and all too aware of what must have caused it—her own foolish reaction, and, of course, the reaction of her husband. And what was she to do now? She could not think. She rose shakily, wanting to see Eric, but not wanting to see him, either—for what could she say?

"Milady."

Laura tensed as she saw Eric's valet standing in the doorway, regarding her gravely. "Yes, Tim, is anything the matter?" she inquired.

He looked uncomfortable. "His Lordship would like to see you, milady; that is, if you are feeling more the thing."

"I am . . . better," Laura told him reluctantly, wishing strongly that she might have been able to give an excuse. Unfortunately that would only be prolonging the evil day. She continued, "I will come immediately. How is he feeling?"

"He is much better now that he can see, milady," the valet told her.

"I am pleased," she murmured as she rose. She was relieved to find that the room was no longer whirling around her, but still she did not feel well, and undoubtedly she would be feeling considerably worse by the time she had explained matters to her husband. And what would *he* say about a pretense that now, in retrospect, seemed utterly mad. Certainly he would be angry, but perhaps he also might be amused. And he had wanted an heir—that was why he had married her. Well, he might have one, and once he knew the truth, surely he would be pleased by at least one outcome of her pretense—at least, she devoutly hoped he would be pleased.

In spite of these comforting thoughts, she hesitated at the door to her husband's room before knocking. Finally she tapped upon that portal, albeit faintly.

"Yes?" Eric called.

"You . . . wanted to see me, Eric," Laura said.

"Yes, madame, I wanted to see you," he said icily. "Please come in."

Laura shivered. She had never heard him use that tone of voice before. She entered and stood at the foot of the bed. Eric was sitting up, propped against several pillows.

His eyes were hard as he stared at her. "I am told, madame," he said in freezing accents, "that you anticipate a child."

Laura swallowed an air bubble in her throat. Obviously he was confused as well as angry. His attitude was going to make her explanation much more difficult, but it must needs be tendered, and along with it, the reasons behind her miserable masquerade, which at this moment seemed mad. "Yes, that is . . . is true, Eric. You see . . ."

"Yes, I do see," he snapped. "I expect I do not need to be told who the father is. Obviously your long hours in the library were not passed entirely in the discovery of old books!"

Laura tensed, staring at him incredulously. "My . . . time in . . . in the library?" she repeated.

"Yes, madame," came the icy response. "Your time in the library. Your sister told me that you and young Mr. Quinn were extremely friendly—or was your paramour a stable boy? I understand you also did a great deal of riding as well. No, I really cannot see you stooping quite that low."

Amazement warred with hurt, and hurt with indignation. "You . . . you are . . . are saying—" she began.

"I am saying," Eric interrupted in freezing accents, "that if you hope to use your marriage as a mask to conceal your bastard, I will not connive at the deception. I am summoning my lawyer, and even though I am much against divorce, I feel that I will have no difficulty in obtaining one—once the judge has heard my story. I have already sent word that your Mr. Quinn is to be dismissed. I have ordered that he leave the premises immediately he is packed!"

"You . . . you dismissed Mr. Quinn?" Laura cried. "But why? He . . . he—"

"I beg you will not waste your time defending him, madame. You, yourself, have acquainted me with the hours you have spent with your . . . your paramour in the library—searching out books for my benefit, is the excuse you gave me."

"The excuse . . ." Laura began. "But, Eric—"

"The excuse, madame," he yelled, bringing one hand down hard on the bed. "Do not tell me that it had anything to do with reading matter. Your sister Julia will bear me out. She, too, remarked upon your affection for . . . for your librarian!"

"She did not!" Laura cried indignantly.

"I beg to differ with you, madame. Your sister was most informative on how you passed your time."

"Oh, really?" Laura was finding that rather than being hurt, she was angry or, rather, furious, as furious as this man on the bed, who had not asked for an explanation, who had only accused her . . . this despite the hours and hours and hours she had spent with him as herself, despite his words of gratitude, which of late had been on the verge of being more than gratitude—or so it had appeared. She continued angrily, "My sister spent a great deal of time in this chamber, my lord, and she left rather precipitately. She avoided speaking to me, and I did not ask her why—but perhaps you have an explanation!"

"Do not try to turn the subject, madame, You and that little . . . oh, God, and while I lay here helpless, I was being *cuckolded* by my wife with . . . with my librarian! It is very difficult to obtain a divorce, but I shall insist upon it. I hope that I will be able to be granted it immediately, or at least within the next eight months, because, madame, I want your disgrace to be common knowledge. I am not going to be the gentleman and accept responsibility for your bastard! Furthermore—"

"I do not think that I wish to hear another word from you, my lord," Laura interrupted with a coldness that exceeded his own. "I will make my own arrangements. I will leave this house within the hour."

"I am pleased that you have not found it necessary to defend yourself, madame," he said furiously. He half rose and then fell back, wincing. "Oh, God, were I not chained to this bed, I would beat you within an inch of your life, and your damned paramour too."

"Then, my lord, we are both extremely fortunate that

you are so indisposed." Laura walked out of the room.
She longed to slam the door, but instead she closed it
quietly. Then, seeing the valet standing outside, looking
at her regretfully, she said, "Has Mr. Quinn left yet?"

"No, milady." He appeared disturbed. "If you would
wait . . . his lordship has a hasty temper, but if I were to
explain—"

Laura interrupted freezingly. "You may find Lucy, if
you will, and also have someone tell Mr. Quinn that I
wish to see him immediately. I will await him in the
library."

"Yes, milady." He paused and seemed on the point of
saying something else, then, with a sigh, he bowed and
hurried away.

Coming into the library, Laura again resisted a strong
impulse to slam the heavy door as hard as she might. She
found herself trembling with an anger that exceeded
anything she had ever experienced in all her eighteen and
a half years. She looked longingly at a pile of books on the
table. To throw them was another impulse she must
needs resist, for it might injure them beyond repair.
Furthermore she did have one outlet for her anger or,
rather, fury. She could leave and would leave immediately the horses could be harnessed. Fortunately it was not
even noon yet, and by nightfall she could be a league or
more away. She would take Eric's traveling coach and
horses. Her mother could send them back. Her thoughts
fled as the door was opened, and Mr. Quinn, pale and
shocked, hurried into the library. He came to a stop as he
saw Laura."

"I-I do not know—" he began shakily.

"Mr. Quinn," Laura interrupted curtly. "You and I
will be leaving together. I quite understand that this
departure will convince my husband of what he appears
to believe already—that we have carried on a long and
clandestine love affair within the confines of the library
—possibly between the bookshelves or under the desk."
A mirthless laugh escaped her. "However, I feel that
given the way word travels around here, you might have

difficulty in finding another position, and our library at home is much in need of your kind offices. When I have explained your situation and mine to my mother, I am sure she will be in agreement with me.

"I have no doubt that the man I married will eventually learn the truth, but I am in no mind to linger here. Will you come with me? I suggest that you do—because until my husband does come to his so-called senses, you will have a difficult time, indeed. However, I think that I am quite safe in saying that your reputation will be easily restored."

The librarian said, "Milady, whether it is or not, I will be glad to accompany you wherever you wish to go—and whether or not there is employment at the end of the journey."

Sudden tears blurred Laura's vision. "You are indeed kind, sir, especially in view of the unmerited tongue-lashing you must have received from his lordship. Are you finished with your packing yet?"

"Very nearly, milady."

"Then when you are completely done, please await me in the stable yard."

Coming into her own chamber, Laura was joined by her pale and shocked abigail. "You . . . you will be leavin' within the hour, milady?"

"Yes," Laura snapped. "You need not take many of my garments, Lucy. No doubt his lordship will be pleased to send them to me. I cannot believe that he will want anything of mine in this house."

"Oh, milady, if you would but explain . . ." Lucy began.

Laura drew herself up. "He did not give me an opportunity to explain, Lucy. He did not wish to hear any explanation from me. He accused me of committing adultery with the librarian. I beg you will not smile. It is no smiling matter."

Lucy bit down her inadvertent grin. "But, milady, how can he possibly—"

"I expect some of his confusion can be laid at my

door," Laura interrupted impatiently. "I would have allowed for confusion, Lucy, but . . ." Laura blinked back tears. "No matter, I am going, Lucy, and there's an end to it. To think that he who . . . with . . . but I have said there's an end to it. Please take what you think I will be needing and let us be on our way."

There was a tap at the door.

"Well?" Laura demanded.

"If you please, milady." The housekeeper hurried in. "His lordship does not understand. If you would but explain . . ."

"I will tell you, as I have just told Lucy," Laura said coldly. "I came with explanations on my lips, but his lordship gave no sign of wishing to hear them. He had reached his decision before I opened the door. You will find the physician in agreement with him, no doubt."

"But, milady, neither of them know . . ."

"Nor did they wish to know. I was convicted before I ever opened Lord Marne's door. If he had had the slightest bit of affection for me, the slightest interest, he would have given me a chance to explain. He did not wish to hear my explanations, and I charge you, do not enlighten him further. No doubt he will want to start proceedings for a divorce as soon as he is on his feet again. Let him do so, for it is obvious that that is what he wishes—and may have wished all along."

"Milady, you do not know him as I—"

"You are quite right. I do not know him, and nor do I wish to know the man who spoke to me as he has just spoken to me," Laura said icily. "I do thank you for all you have done, Mrs. Wilson. I leave his lordship in your capable hands, and now—farewell."

"Oh, milady." Mrs. Wilson wrung her capable hands. "He . . . he ought to know the truth."

"Mrs. Wilson, I do not wish him to know the truth," Laura said coldly. "I know the sort of gossip that circulates through the various mansions. I would prefer that if possible, you and the staff will not add to it. In fact, I would like your word, at least, that *you* will not."

The housekeeper sighed. "You have my word, milady."

"And will you please see if you can exact similar promises from the staff?"

"I will do my best, milady."

"I thank you, and I also thank you for all that you have done for me while I was here. You will hear from me once I have reached my mother's house. If his lordship desires to know the whereabouts of his librarian, you may tell him that Mr. Quinn has gone with me. I assure you that he will not be surprised."

"Oh, milady, I do wish you Godspeed." Mrs. Wilson's eyes brimmed with tears.

"I thank you, Mrs. Wilson," Laura repeated.

His leg was hurting, and a headache pounded at his temples. The white heat of his rage had lessened. In its place was pain, a pain that had nothing to do with his physical discomfort. In the last three weeks he had come to care for his wife to the point that he bitterly regretted the episode with her sister, and on numerous occasions the truth had risen in his mind and begged to be transmitted to his tongue, but he had not wanted to rend the delicate fabric of this new relationship which was beginning to mean so very much to him, so much more than he had ever anticipated!

Each morning he had looked forward to Laura's arrival in his chamber. She had spent a great deal of the day with him, and often she had come to him in the night, offering her comfort when he was beset by pain or by fears that he might not see again. She had reminded him of the doctor's words, and she had also told him of others who had suffered similarly and recovered easily.

She had such a beautiful voice, much more beautiful than that of her sister Julia, whom he never wanted to see again, her adulterous sister—but they were both adulterous . . . Laura and the librarian!

He shuddered and groaned. How could she have gone from his chamber to that man? That was what she must have done, for their unholy alliance could never have happened during the day. The servants would have found them out and told him. No, it had taken place during the

long reaches of the night. He could see it in his mind's
eye, Mr. Quinn lying in her bed while she came to tend
the man she called husband—only to go back to *him*.
And where was she now?

He had the answer to that—tendered to him by
Wilson, who had come to tell him that Laura had
gone—taking the traveling coach and sharing it with Mr.
Quinn, her lover! Consequently it was useless to long for
the welcome sound of her step in the corridor . . . but it
was not welcome! She had done the unthinkable, the
unforgivable! Denied the attentions of himself, she had
accepted those of his librarian, had yielded her virginity
to his librarian, and now was fleeing with her lover . . .
where? It did not matter, she did not matter, nothing
mattered anymore. Eric buried his face in his pillow, and
in his weakness he could not hold back his tears.

"Then it's true? She is gone and not one word for me?"
Lady Orville bent a smoldering eye on Mrs. Wilson.
They were standing in the front hall of Marne Castle.
"Come, Mrs. Wilson," she continued. "You know why,
do you not—and if you will tell me she left with her lover
and further tell me that he is none other than that measly
librarian, then I will tell *you* that you are as mad as my
informant. There is more here than meets the eye and
ear. The *on dit* is so garbled that I can make neither head
nor tail of it. Unfortunately I was bedded with a quinsy
for a fortnight, else I would have been here sooner. God,
what a time to suffer a quinsy! Come, Mrs. Wilson, and
do not try my patience by telling me that it was Mr.
Quinn who got her with child!"

The housekeeper reddened. "Your l-ladyship!"

"Have none of you told him the truth, the truth I am
positive you know as well as I myself?"

"She made us swear that we would not. I have never
seen her so exercised, milady. She left that same afternoon."

"And why would she not?" Lady Orville demanded
crossly. She loosed another sigh. "Two weeks . . . two

bloody weeks, I beg your pardon, Mrs. Wilson, but by God, had I been myself, I could have put matters to right in a moment. Damn the girl—all she needed to do was tell him the truth."

"I think she . . . she might have been primed to give him that truth, milady," Mrs. Wilson said reluctantly, "but he was in no mind to hear it. He did all the talking."

"And judging from what you or someone else was able to hear, he said a very great deal!"

"A very great deal, your ladyship." The housekeeper sighed. "To Mr. Quinn also—and him, poor young gentleman, not having the slightest notion what his lordship meant."

"Of course he would not," Lady Orville snapped. "And then Laura put more coals on the fire by asking Mr. Quinn to accompany her to her home. As it happens, I fault neither her judgment nor her spirit! I think I would have done the same in her place, but I never would have been in her place. Whenever my husband is ill and cross as a bear, I turn him over to the servants."

"Yes, your ladyship."

"What can you be meaning by 'Yes, your ladyship,' Mrs. Wilson? Oh, I think I know. You are suggesting that my high-handed ways with man and beast do not go unobserved. Nothing goes unobserved in these parts, which is why I want the truth from you regarding her ladyship. I have a strong feeling that she went home."

"Yes, Lady Orville, she did. And that is why she had Mr. Quinn accompany her, I am sure. He is without a position, poor young gentleman, and she suggested that he could work in her library at home."

"How very like Laura. She is kindness itself—anyone else tarred with that sort of a brush never would have offered him a position for fear of all the idle gossip that entertains those of us who are idle. And she was more than kind to his lordship, as I am sure you know."

"Oh, Lady Orville, we do. . . ." The housekeeper sighed.

"And where is his lordship at present?"

"He is walking in the garden."

"Ah, he is able to walk, then."

"Yes, even though he does tire easily. But he is determined to get the use of his limb and his ankle back—despite the advice of Mr. Chatterton."

"I will go and speak to him," Lady Orville said determinedly.

Mrs. Wilson regarded her anxiously, and then she smiled. "I will show you where he usually rests," she said.

Naturally Mrs. Wilson did not take Lady Orville all the way to the spot where his lordship might be found. Instead she showed her the path that lay by a tall yew hedge. "On the other side there's a fish pond. He was fond of it as a lad, and there's a stone bench nearby. Of late, whenever he's tired, it seems to calm his nerves to look into that pool." Mrs. Wilson lowered her voice. "He don't much like being disturbed there."

"I understand," Lady Orville said in equally low tones, "but every so often a disturbance is necessary . . . to make us aware of things which might escape us and which should not."

"To be sure, milady," the housekeeper murmured. She added, "Lady Laura is much missed, and I think not only by the staff, milady."

Lady Orville nodded. "I do not see how it could be any other way, Mrs. Wilson. I miss her myself. And I do thank you."

She moved up the indicated path, and coming to a break between the hedges, she glimpsed the pool. It was round, and on the brink there was a small, lovely bronze figure—a dancing goddess. Nearby was the marble bench Mrs. Wilson had mentioned. Lady Orville was disappointed to find it unoccupied, but even as she started to turn away, she saw a shadow fall across the path leading to the pool, and in another moment Eric appeared. He was limping rather badly, and it was with an expression of relief that he sank down on the bench, rubbing his ankle, which appeared to be still swollen, and next his leg. Then he sighed and stared moodily into the pool.

Lady Orville moved onto the path between the hedges. "Good afternoon, Eric," she called cheerily. "I was told you were up and about. I am so pleased." Meeting a dark and undeniably resentful gaze, she smiled brightly. "You do look better, I must say. But it was a very long siege, was it not? Poor Laura was beside herself with anxiety. I understand that she had gone to see her mother. Do you plan to join her, my dear?"

He glared at her. "I think that you must be quite aware that I do not . . . and I am sure you must know why, Lady Orville, and having said that, I do not believe that we need prolong this conversation."

"Dear, dear, you do seem to be in a bearish mood. It is the same with my husband. If he sustains an injury, no matter how small, he develops fangs, claws, and a growl. However, my dear Eric, I have a great deal to say to you regarding your wife."

"I do not wish to hear it!" he snapped. Rising swiftly, he turned away, and the movement being too quick for his present condition, he stumbled and fell.

"Oh, dear." Lady Orville knelt beside him. "Your poor leg . . . does it hurt? Or was it your ankle that threw you?"

"No . . . and please, I . . . I beg you will leave me alone," he said with a groan.

"You are still in considerable pain, I see. I am sorry for that," she said. Then, moving closer to him, she sat down on the grass and eased his leg onto her lap. "I think that I can make it feel a little better, my dear Eric."

"My man is nearby. I will call him," Eric said raspily.

"Oh, my poor Eric, I know he is not. Furthermore, I also know that you are wont to come here and commune with nature or, more accurately, brood in silence, but I think you must hear what I am determined to tell you."

"If it is about La— If it is about my wife, I do not want to hear it." He glared at her. "And," he continued, before she could respond, "I imagine that you are her confidante, and as such, I am not interested in anything you might have to say."

"If I were as sensitive as poor Laura, I suppose I would withdraw, but, my dearest Eric, I am not." Lady Orville continued to run her hands over his leg. "My gracious, the muscles in your calf are tense . . . let me massage them. Bruce thinks me particularly adept at easing tight muscles and banishing pain. Often after a hunt he becomes my patient. Now"—she began to massage his leg,—"does that not feel a little more the thing?"

Again Eric, without success, tried to pull away from a hold as tenacious as her speech. "I tell you I can call my man!" he snapped.

"And I will tell you that before you do, I think you must hear something from me that will no doubt astound you, and which, my dear, is a great deal more believable than Laura's supposed dalliance with little Mr. Quinn. Are you quite mad, Eric? Can you imagine that Laura would affix horns to your head with a . . . a traveling librarian? You must have a mighty poor opinion of yourself, and an even worse one of her."

He glared at her and again tried to pull away from her, but without success. "Did . . . did she then receive her . . . anticipated infant from the angel who visited the Virgin Mary?" he demanded sarcastically.

Lady Orville clicked her tongue. "Gracious, Eric, this is not an age of miracles, or perhaps it is, for it does seem entirely miraculous to me that you have not yet guessed the truth. . . . No, on second thought, it is not quite that miraculous. You might have been confused—given their voices."

"Their voices . . ." he echoed. "What are you babbling about?"

Lady Orville continued to massage his leg. "There, my dear, does that not feel a little better? I am speaking about your limb, Eric."

"Damn my limb," he said rudely. "What did you mean?"

"Worse and worse, but I will forgive you, though I do

not believe Laura should have been quite so forgiving, given your reprehensible actions with her 'sister.'"

Eric's leg grew quite rigid. "Her . . . her sister? I do not understand. What can you mean?"

"I am talking about her beautiful sister Julia, of whom you seemed to be extremely fond."

"What do you know about Julia?" he demanded tensely.

"Actually I know far too much about her and, at the same time, not quite enough. She is quite lovely to look at, and that is amazing. Most women of her age begin to show their characters in their faces. Julia, however, has been more fortunate. She remains quite beautiful—and that, despite her essential hardness and selfishness."

"Julia . . . selfish?" he echoed on a note of angry protest. "She is not selfish, she—"

Lady Orville interrupted, saying coolly, "I must disagree with you, Eric, dear. I think it quite uncommonly selfish to leave you the day after the accident, especially since you had been so friendly before the lighting of the bonfire. Goodness, Eric, dear, relax. Your leg is all tied up in knots again."

"Damn my leg!" he burst out. "What can you . . . you mean? J-Julia did not leave me after the accident. She . . . she was very k-kind, only I wish . . . but never mind that." He glared at her. "You are entirely mistaken, Lady Orville. She did not leave me."

"Oh, yes, my dear Eric, she did. She quarreled with Laura, who did not want her to go, though I must admit that I was the culprit here. I suggested to Julia, whom I really cannot abide, that she leave. She was very quick to take advantage of that suggestion. In fact, she left the next morning."

"But she . . . she came to me that night," he cried confusedly.

"No, my dear, she did not. That was Laura. Their voices are very similar, which is often the way with sisters. You are probably not aware of that, since you have only the one sister."

"B-but later, she . . . she must have returned. She did return." Eric stared at her in consternation.

"No, my dear Eric." Lady Orville spoke gently. "Julia has not been seen around these parts since the morning after the bonfire. She left very early. It was shortly after the rising of the sun."

He had turned very pale, and his eyes were wide. "But I . . . but we . . . oh, God, Lady Orville, what are you telling me?"

Lady Orville spoke slowly, purposely weighting her words. "I am telling you, my dear Eric, that I am your wife's only confidante, and that she was dreadfully upset because Julia had gone, and she felt you would be miserably disappointed. Consequently she used her voice to what she believed to be good effect. I tried to persuade her that eventually she must run into trouble, but she would not listen. None of my arguments swayed her, and furthermore, she begged the household staff to cooperate, and they did. They, in common with your wife, were most concerned over your state of mind."

"And . . . and the child?" he asked hoarsely.

"The child was conceived upon a night when you persuaded a reluctant 'Julia' to lie with you . . . and because you were so persuasive and so needful, Eric, my dear, she, who could deny you nothing, did not deny you that. Oh, my dear," Lady Orville said with a burst of compassion as the man before her lifted his hands and, covering his face, began to sob loudly and as brokenly as a lost and terrified child.

NINE

DESPITE THE FACT that his servants had been adjured not to reveal his wife's strange masquerade, Eric at first found it hard to forgive what he could not help feel was deep disloyalty—especially on the part of the Wilsons and his valet! They should have told him. Yet if they had, what would his reaction have been? That question had been put to him by Lady Orville. She had also delegated herself to provide his answer.

"You would have been angry and embarrassed, my dear. Furthermore, in your condition, such knowledge must have weighed very heavily upon you. Believe me, it was best that you did not know, which is what Laura believed. I am quite sure, however, that she was primed to tell you . . . immediately after the doctor left, was indeed steeling herself to give you the truth. . . ."

"And I would not listen," he had said crossly. "I would have been angry with my servants also," he had subsequently admitted, surprising her, he knew. Lady Orville did not have a very high opinion of him, he feared. He was surprised by the regret that came with this realization. Despite his fondness for Bruce, his longtime comrade, and his early liking for her as well, Christina had managed to prejudice him against her, and he thought he knew why.

Christina never would have appreciated Lady Orville's frankness. Indeed, Christina and some truths were strangers, he knew. Time and time again he had heard her telling people what she believed they wanted to hear rather than the less palatable truths they should have heard.

Had not Laura done the same?

No, she had only wanted to spare his feelings. Christina had lived a secret life inside her head, one to which he never had access. Laura was by nature frank and kind. Now, knowing all, he realized ruefully that he had never experienced such kindness! With all her falsehoods, she had been strictly on the side of the angels, endeavoring to protect him from knowledge that she feared must wound him deeply, and consequently she had used the voice she shared with Julia or, rather, the voice that Julia shared with her. Julia was only a pallid shadow of the reality that was Laura. It was this woman with whom he had fallen in love, this woman who called herself Julia but who had been Laura, and then he had learned that he loved Laura, herself, even more. He must see her, explain his confusion and beg her pardon, most *abjectly* beg her pardon!

A new fear enveloped him as he contemplated this journey in which he would not be able to embark for at least a fortnight. Would Laura be willing to speak to him, and would she ever, ever forgive him?

Lady Roswell took a turn around the back parlor and came to where the countess was sitting. She loosed a deep sigh. "I tell you, I do not know the child. She has received two more letters from Eric, and as usual she has torn them both in two without reading them. They were long letters, too, from the look of the scraps."

The countess clicked her tongue. "Could you not have pieced them together, Dorothy?"

"I would have tried, but she burned them in the kitchen fire."

"I have never known the child to be so stubborn." The countess sighed.

"Nor I." Lady Roswell groaned.

"Still, she does look amazingly well. In fact, I have never seen her looking so well—in spite of her gloomy frame of mind and her condition," the countess observed. "And even though she is breeding, she has matured, and in my estimation she is quite as lovely as Julia."

"I beg you will not mention Julia to me," snapped Lady Roswell. "I have half a mind to black her name out of the family Bible!"

"You should have done that years ago. I told you—"

"You told me nothing!" snapped her ladyship with pardonable indignation. "You thought there was none who could hold a candle to Julia—and she *is* beautiful."

"I do not countenance the idea of her playing fast and loose with her own brother-in-law, certainly," the countess retorted.

Lady Roswell rolled her eyes and sighed. "It is a habit of hers. When she visited Margaret in Scotland, she was quite taken with the laird."

"And he?" the countess snapped.

"He did not return the compliment, thanks be to God. Margaret tells me that he only laughed at her stratagems —with the result that she cut short her visit with a complaint about the Scottish mists. Unfortunately Eric was more susceptible."

"Young rascal!" snapped the countess. "He is not worth one of poor Laura's tears."

"She has not been weeping. She is dry-eyed and cold."

"Indeed?" The countess frowned. "That, my dear, is not a good sign."

"I am only too aware of that."

"What does she do with her days since she cannot go riding?"

"She spends a great deal of time in the library with young Mr. Quinn. He is a most accomplished librarian and scholar. And I can assure you that he has his work cut out for him in our library."

"I am certainly not surprised at that," the countess said tartly. "I imagine that save for Laura's visits, it has not been touched since the death of my poor son."

Before Lady Roswell could comment, she added, "Laura cannot be interested in Mr. Quinn, can she?"

"No, but they are good friends, and she does like to read."

"Does she do nothing else?"

"She walks in the garden, but more often she sits by the stream. She has always loved the woods."

"How is her mood in general?"

"It is very hard to tell. She has become extremely closemouthed. She is not the same girl she used to be. Oh, dear . . . do you know, I am quite sure that she intends to divorce young Eric."

"Good heavens, are you sure?"

"I am afraid I am."

"He will never agree to it. There has never been such a scandal in his family or our own."

"It was he who suggested it in the first place." Lady Roswell sighed.

"That, of course, being before he learned the truth," the countess said. "There will be no divorce."

"Laura has asked me to write to Mr. Prentice, who is—"

"I know who he is. Do you imagine that you are talking to a stranger? You will do no such thing."

"I have told her that he is away, and she has said that she will make inquiries and find another lawyer. She wishes to divorce Eric as soon as possible. I have told her what everyone will believe, and she has told me that she does not care what they believe." Lady Roswell sighed. "I tell you, I no longer know her!"

The countess glared at her. "Something must prevent this scandal! Has she no sense of the proprieties?"

"None," Lady Roswell said grimly.

"I cannot believe that she has lost all feeling for young Eric," the countess said.

"It appears that she has. I do not know her, I tell you. And—" She broke off hastily as Laura appeared in the doorway. "My dear, here is your grandmother," Lady Roswell said unnecessarily.

"Good afternoon, Laura, dear," the countess said. She

added with some surprise, "My dear, you are looking very well."

"I thank you, Grandmother." Laura smiled, but it was an expression that found no answering gleam in eyes, the coldness of which startled the countess.

"Well, my dear, I am told you are increasing."

"Yes, that is true, Grandmother," Laura responded. "I will bear the child in something under seven months, the doctor informs me. I am in hopes that it will be a girl."

"One never knows," the countess said. "I hope you will not be too disappointed if it proves to be a boy."

"I expect that I have no choice in the matter." Laura shrugged.

"I have received yet another letter from—" Lady Roswell began.

"If you are about to tell me that you have heard from my husband again, Mama, I am not interested," Laura said freezingly.

"My dear, I have told you that in the last letter he wrote to me—"

"Please, Mama." Laura held up an impatient hand. "I have said I am not interested."

"But, my dear Laura," the countess protested, "if your husband is willing to let bygones be bygones—"

"If he is willing," Laura interrupted yet again, "I am not willing, for there are no bygones."

"It was a pardonable error," the countess persisted despite her daughter-in-law's sharp nudge.

"I do not find it pardonable, Grandmother."

"Would you prefer that your child be considered a bastard?" the countess demanded.

"Yes, I would much prefer that, Grandmother." Laura turned and walked out of the room.

"Well, I never . . ." the countess began angrily.

"Oh, dear, you have only added more fuel to her fires." Lady Roswell sighed. "I have told you that he is coming. Could you not have—"

"Are you daring to reproach *me?*" the countess demanded in ascending anger.

"Yes, I am," Lady Roswell said crossly. "I gave you fair

warning concerning Laura's state of mind, and you should have held your peace."

"Well!" The countess rose and took a turn around the room. "I hardly need to answer for my actions to you, Dorothy, and unless I have an apology from you in writing, I do not believe we will see each other soon again. I might add that I was planning to bestow a certain sum upon each of my granddaughters, but in the circumstances, there is my late husband's family to consider too."

"I beg you will bestow your money wherever you think fit," Lady Roswell retorted coldly. "We will not be in want—any of us. You seem to forget that you made certain that all of your sons married heiresses."

"Well," the countess repeated, glaring at her, "I am leaving."

"I will have Peters summon your coach." Lady Roswell also rose.

The countess stood in the middle of the room, a very pretty room decorated in shades of blue and with a most beautifully painted ceiling. She glared at the ceiling, and it had its usual effect on her. "Oh, damn and blast it, Dorothy," she said sharply. "Let us both calm down and put our heads together rather than our fists at each other's eyes. That silly girl cannot wreck the rest of her life in this careless fashion. When is that young cub arriving?"

Tears stood in Lady Roswell's eyes. "He . . . he should be here within a day or two. He must travel by slow stages, he wrote me. I have the impression that he is far from well—even now."

"That pleases me," the countess said.

"It pleases you?" Lady Roswell regarded her with considerable surprise.

"Yes, I know that Laura is deeply hurt, but I suspect that her hurt is based on her deep love for him rather than from any lack of that emotion. If he is not at his best and he is truly repentent . . . that is an excellent combination."

"Oh, I do hope you are right." Lady Roswell sighed.

"I will consult Jane," the countess promised.

"Please . . ." Lady Roswell murmured. "And I am sorry that I was rude."

"I beg you will accept my apologies, my dear Dorothy. I know that you are overwrought, and so am I . . . and we both should retain our calm and sanity, especially at this time."

"I do agree," Lady Roswell said. She added bitterly, "Oh, that I had Julia here, I would certainly give her a piece of my mind."

"Let us both be grateful that she is not here, Dorothy."

"Indeed." Her daughter-in-law sighed.

It had taken close on four days to traverse the one hundred and forty odd miles that lay between Chard and Norwich, the town that lay nearest to Roswell Manor. His coach was well-sprung and his horses were fleet. Furthermore, the changes he received on the road were equally fleet, but unfortunately Eric was obliged to travel far more slowly than pleased him, given what might await him at his journey's end. Unfortunately the time was lengthened by an unexpected and steady downpour that rendered travel impossible for two days. Now, however, they were beyond a lengthy stretch of fields and woods and were, at last, approaching Roswell Manor, an estate that the landlord of the inn in which he had spent the night had praised, telling him that it was a house that had been originally built at the end of Elizabeth's reign but that there had been various additions over the centuries, and these all in keeping with the existing architecture.

Though Eric had always been interested in such survivals, the thought of the manor meant only that finally he would have reached his journey's end and that he would see and hopefully convince Laura that he loved her more than life—and that that same life would mean precious little to him were she not to return home with him.

The house lay some distance from the inn, and also

some distance from the gates. As his coach wound up a road bordered by a variety of trees and bushes, he was even more fearful, on unwillingly recalling his last meeting with her, that she would not see him. Had he really spoken so harshly to her? There was no denying that he had accused her of conducting a love affair with poor little Mr. Quinn. Even more unwillingly he remembered the librarian's astonished face and his stuttering, shocked rebuttal of those accusations, and his own anger as he had cried, "You do your lady great harm in this, my lord."

What had he said in return? He had furiously ordered him out, telling him to leave within the hour, had called him "scoundrel" and had threatened him with prison— had he also mentioned a horsewhipping? He had. Subsequently he had hurled even more heinous accusations at poor Laura, and seen her face change from concern to misery and, at the last, to anger, an anger which, according to her mother's letter, still smoldered and showed no signs of abating.

"I have never seen the child in such a taking," Lady Roswell had written. "I have never known her to harbor anger for so long. I have tried my best to intercede for you, but she adamantly refuses to listen. Of late, I have not dared to mention your name. She is obdurate."

That last missive had reached him on the day of his departure. Thinking of it, he released a long, quavering breath and found moisture in his eyes again, wishing, as he had wished every day since Lady Orville had told him the bitter, bitter truth, that he had listened to her. Unfortunately he had not listened; he had only accused, and with such words as still seared his brain for each of them had been unforgivable, and were he in Laura's place, he would not have forgiven himself, either, and if she did not, life would not be worth living.

His lips twisted into a wry smile. He had once imagined that he could not live without Christina, but he had managed, and he had been granted an even greater love—one that he had not recognized until it was too late. Was it really too late? He stared out of the window, hoping that he might see her . . . but though there were workers on the lawn and in the portions of the gardens that he could see, she was not there.

The coach stopped before the great paneled front door set deeply into the redbrick facade of the mansion. Alighting stiffly and with the much-needed help of his valet, Eric moved toward the door. The knocker, fashioned in the shape of a sailing ship, was cold against his hand. He thrust it against its plate and thought that the sound it made was ominous—a knell rather than a summons.

The door was opened quickly by a tall man in dark livery, who regarded him out of chilly gray eyes. He gave his name and was respectfully ushered into a hall full of refracted light from the mullioned windows. The floor was of black-and-white marble, and on either side of a fireplace set in a black marble frame were elaborately carved wooden panels. Above him, he saw a minstrel's gallery, also elaborately carved. A long table of polished walnut stretched to one side of him. He approved the furnishings. He had always liked Tudor houses, and he thought, with a melancholy satisfaction, that it was a proper background for Laura, and possibly it was also one to which she had been very glad to return, given all that had befallen her since she had gone to London and beyond.

"My lord"—the butler coughed slightly—"would you care to follow me?"

"Oh, yes, of course." Eric said, startled out of his unhappy reflections.

A few minutes later, coming into a large, beautifully furnished drawing room, he looked hopefully about him, wondering if he would see Laura. Even though she would hardly welcome him, the sight of *her* would be as refreshing to him as water in the middle of a dry and sunburned desert.

However, the woman who arose from a long golden sofa as he entered was not Laura. It was Lady Roswell, of course, and while she smiled at him pleasantly enough, she was not quite able to vanquish a look of concern that might also be interpreted as one of regret. Her concern appeared to increase as she regarded him more closely.

"You have lost quite a bit of weight, Eric, dear," she said in lieu of a greeting, and evidently uncomfortably aware of that, she added, "I am pleased to see you again."

"I thank you, Lady Roswell," he said, forcing a smile. "I am pleased to be here. And yes, I have lost some weight, I expect. One cannot always dine well on a long journey."

"Of course not," she agreed. "It is one reason why I really loathe long journeys. Will you not sit down, Eric." She indicated a chair near the couch.

"I thank you, Lady Roswell," he said as he carefully sat down, needing now to rest his ankle, which was still sore, and his leg as well.

"You are feeling more yourself, I trust," she said a second later, breaking the brief silence that had fallen between them.

"Yes, I am totally recovered," he said strongly.

"I am glad to hear it. You were fortunate."

"Fortunate?" he echoed. "Oh, you mean that my injuries were relatively slight?"

"Yes, that is what I meant. You might have been crippled for life, you know."

"Yes, I expect I was . . . fortunate." It was time to ask the question he did not wish to ask but must ask, even though her attitude suggested a negative response. He cleared his throat. "Is she still of the same mind, Lady Roswell?"

"Yes, Eric, I regret to say that she is."

Since he had anticipated as much, he could hardly feel so disappointed, but the weight of that disappointment was heavy on his heart. "If . . . she could understand what I . . . I b-believed," he said helplessly.

"She is aware of what you believed, Eric."

"But how could I know, Lady Roswell?" he burst out. "The doctor told me that she was expecting a child, and

I . . . well, it was a great shock when I thought . . ." He paused, looking at her helplessly.

"I do understand." A long sigh escaped her. "You believed that there could be but one explanation for her condition."

"Precisely." He nodded.

"Unfortunately, my dear Eric, your accusations came on top of all the weeks she had spent nursing you, and of course she was not ignorant of your infatuation for Julia."

"Oh, God." He groaned and ran his hands through his hair. "I do want you to know, Lady Roswell, that it went no further than enjoying her company—at least at first. Then, when she began to spend so many hours in my chamber—or so I believed—she . . . she seemed so different, so concerned and kind and . . . Laura appeared to be gone so much, riding or . . . in the library. It was then that I became drawn to J-Julia. I had never realized that she could be so kind. Afterward, when she appeared to leave and Laura came to take her place . . . I mean, when she, Laura, remained with me all the time, I became very fond of her. Indeed, I grew to love her with all my heart and to bitterly regret that night when Julia, as I believed, came to me. And then . . ." He groaned. "But I am sure you are not ignorant of what ultimately happened."

Lady Roswell sighed. "No, I know what happened, and I do understand your confusion, Eric, but if only you would have given Laura a chance to explain."

"I know . . . I know," he burst out. "I have gone over those moments of my anger so often, and I can no more excuse them in myself than can she. My only defense is that it was a great shock and that I . . . I did not know the truth. And I had come to love her so very deeply." He brushed a hand over his eyes. "Lady Roswell, I . . . I am in agony, and there are times when I fear I shall die of this."

"Oh, Eric, my dear," she said compassionately, "I want to help you, but my daughter, I do not know her or, rather, I think I do. There is more to this situation than appears on the surface. Much as I used to remonstrate with Julia, she was always so cruel to Laura, so mocking and horrid. She did not restrain herself, not even on your wedding day. And, of course, later, when she threw herself on your mercy, as it were—you did appear to give her more comfort than was absolutely necessary."

"I know . . . it was her resemblance to Christina, my late wife that beguiled me, but I . . . I never gave her the attention she seemed to crave, not then." He ran his hands through his hair. "Oh, God, God, what madness this is."

"Yes, madness, indeed. Laura certainly shares the blame for what ultimately happened—yet she did it for you, and it must have been a chore, indeed, knowing what she thought she knew regarding your feeling for Julia—to assume her sister's mask, as it were. And then, when she was about to tell you the truth, was steeling herself to tell you a truth she feared you would find most unpalatable—and explain, too, about the child, you . . ." She spread her hands and shook her head. "You can understand what happened, I am sure."

"I do understand!" he cried. "It was Lady Orville who gave me the truth of the matter—but you know that, too. When the doctor . . . but I have already told you my feelings."

"I do understand. I . . . have given my promise to Laura that on no account will I insist that she see you. She is determined not to see you, Eric. She has sworn that she never wishes to see you again." She held up her hand as he seemed about to interrupt her. "Heed me, my dear. She has *not* exacted one promise from me." Lady Roswell lowered her voice. "Laura is in the habit of taking long walks, and generally she goes to a place that has been her favorite since childhood. It is a swift-flowing stream that runs through our woods. There is a great oak tree at one turn, where Laura usually sits. If it is a fair day tomorrow, she will be there. She is there every day."

"Do you think . . ." he began tentatively.

"I do not think anything, Eric, my dear. In a sense I have betrayed a confidence, and my daughter as well, save that she did not precisely confide in me, at least in regards to that stream and that oak." Lady Roswell gave him a brief smile. "Meanwhile, my lad, I strongly suggest that you find an inn nearby and rest. It is obvious to me that you are still not in your best physical condition, and I am sure that the journey here was wearing. Furthermore, I have a strong feeling that Laura was observing the arrival and will be anticipating the departure of your coach. I will offer further aid in the guise of an assurance that you were much discouraged by what I told you regarding her state of mind. I will let her make what she chooses out of that."

"You are suggesting that she will believe me gone home?" he asked hopefully.

"I think it is best that I do not refine further on what I have already told you, my dear Eric." Her ladyship rose and held out her hand.

Rising, Eric bent to kiss it. "I will say farewell for the nonce," he said in a low voice. "And I do thank you."

"I will echo your farewell, my dear Eric, and hope for the best."

Shortly after Eric's coachman had guided the vehicle back in the direction of the road to Norwich, Laura came slowly down the stairs. A few minutes later she had joined her mother in the drawing room. "He has gone?" she inquired coolly.

"Yes, my dear," Lady Roswell responded.

"You persuaded him that it was useless to return, I hope, Mama?"

"I gave him your sentiments, my dear. You know, Laura, he is extremely cast down."

"Indeed? Then you must advise him to seek out Julia, now that he is well. I am sure that she will be only too delighted to help raise his flagging spirits, Mama."

"Laura!" Lady Roswell protested. "You cannot mean what you are saying."

"Why would I not mean it?" Laura questioned coldly. "Eric is extremely fond of Julia. That goes without saying."

"Then I strongly suggest, my dear, that you do not say it," Lady Roswell snapped. "Eric was very fond of *your* version of Julia, and I might add that he appeared extremely cast down by your uncompromising attitude. And—"

"I do not wish to discuss the matter, Mama. I wish only to hear that you have given him my sentiments on this situation."

"As I have already told you, I have."

"I do thank you, Mama. May I be allowed to hope that he has returned to Somerset?"

"He did not acquaint me with his destination, my dear. Suffice to say that he took your strictures much to heart and has gone. Now, I think it were better if you were to lie down. You are looking very pale."

"It is my condition and nothing more, Mama," Laura told her defensively.

"Of course, my dear, and if that condition is predicated on your husband's departure, surely it must improve, and soon."

"I am feeling more the thing already," Laura assured her strongly. "Will you excuse me, Mama?"

"Of course, my dear."

Laura walked slowly up the stairs. She had not been precisely accurate when she had told her mother that she was feeling better. She did have hopes of feeling better, but meanwhile the morning sickness she had been experiencing had, as usual, lasted well beyond the midday meal, which she had lost shortly after partaking of it. She felt really wretched, and as she sank down on her bed she also found herself oddly disappointed.

It seemed to her that scarcely had her husband arrived than he had taken his leave. Obviously her mother had done her work well and he had been discouraged. She had not, however, expected that he would be discouraged quite so easily, especially given the flood of letters that he had sent to her and which, of course, she had not read. She had half a mind to join Mr. Quinn in the library, but the other half of her mind demanded that she remain where she was, and if there was a certain wetness in her eyes, it was due to her condition. Indeed, she thought indignantly, the fact that he would come here after all that had occurred was one more example of his inordinate conceit!

"How dare he imagine that I would ever forgive him?" she whispered angrily.

An image of Eric arose in her mind's eye and was furiously blinked away. "I will never forgive him," she said firmly. "I would rather die!"

It occurred to her that women occasionally did die in childbirth. "Perhaps I will," she whispered, and found the notion oddly appealing until she realized that it would save Eric the expense and the difficulties attendant upon a divorce.

"I will not die," she muttered, and buried her face in her pillows, hoping that sleep would come quickly and that she would be feeling more herself when she awoke. She usually felt better in the late afternoon.

On the morning after Eric's surprisingly brief visit, Laura woke after a troubled, dream-filled night. She had a small repast of chocolate and rolls. When Lucy came to take away the tray, she said, albeit very casually, "I do not expect that Lord Marne returned here last night."

"No, milady, he did not," Lucy said.

"Ah, I am pleased." Laura smiled. "I think I will go for a little walk this morning—since it appears to be a fair day."

"Very good, milady," Lucy said. "What will you wear? It will be another warm morning, I believe."

"It does not matter." Laura shrugged. "I am only going for a walk. I do not intend to meet anyone."

"The sprigged muslin, milady?"

"That will do well enough." Laura nodded. "I expect most of my gowns will need to be let out eventually."

"In another month or so, milady."

"I expect you know that . . . that my husband came here yesterday."

"Yes, milady, and has already gone." Lucy nodded.

"Yes, he must be well on his way back to Somerset by now. At least I hope he is."

"I expect he is, milady," Lucy murmured.

"I am really amazed that he would have the temerity to come here, after all that has taken place."

"It does seem surprising, milady," Lucy commented.

"I have not answered a single one of his letters. I have torn them up without reading them, and on two occasions I sent the pieces back to him. One would imagine that that must have discouraged him from coming here. It is a very long journey for anyone to take for nothing, do you not agree, Lucy?"

"I expect that he hoped it would not be for nothing, milady."

Laura turned blazing eyes on Lucy, almost as if she were the culprit in question. "I do not see how he could have dared to . . . to expect that I . . . after what he said . . . Really, Lucy, his effrontery passes all understanding."

Lucy said carefully, "I have noticed that gentlemen do not think the way we do."

"Certainly they do not, Lucy," Laura snapped. "To . . . to accuse me of . . . of . . . I begin to believe that they do not think at all!"

"That is entirely possible, milady. Do you wish to rise now?"

"Yes, I will." Laura slipped out of bed and then was obliged to steady herself by holding on to one of the posts as the room seemed to circle around her.

Lucy said quickly, "Would you care to lie down again, milady?"

The room had suddenly righted. "No, I am better. And it looks to be a fine day. There's hardly a cloud in the sky. The weather is much better here than in Somerset, do you not agree, Lucy?"

"I have not thought much about it, milady, but possibly it is."

"I would say that it is definitely better here. The winds are not so strong."

"No, milady."

Actually, by the time that Laura, clad in her sprigged muslin and carrying Jane Austen's *Northanger Abbey,* obtained after a lengthy search through the library shelves, Mr. Quinn being unaccountably absent, started toward her favorite spot in the woods, a strong breeze had sprung up. However, though it blew her hair out of Lucy's careful arrangement and swirled her skirts about her legs, it did not deter her from seeking her destination.

It had occurred to Laura that there was a distinct possibility that his lordship might make an effort to see her yet again, and while he might even dare to search for her on the grounds, he would certainly not come to the woods. She would remain by the stream most of the morning, her absence would discourage him, and he would return to Somerset if, indeed, he had not already done so, which she hoped he had.

As usual it was with a feeling of great pleasure that Laura sank down in front of the great oak tree that had been her favorite spot all the days of her life. In other years she had climbed it to sit in a hollow place formed by three branches. That, of course, was impossible at present. She grimaced, thinking of the reason why she must needs abstain from climbing trees, and much to her confusion, and subsequently her anger, she was forced to blink away the tears that had unaccountably risen to blur her vision. It was entirely ridiculous to weep over the plight in which she now found herself. One ought to have *pride,* certainly! She passed a hand over her eyes, crossly wiping away her foolish tears. Then, opening her book, one she had read many times before, she turned to one of her favorite spots and read once again how the heroine Catherine had mistaken a laundry list for a mysterious communication.

"It is very kind of you to show me the way," Eric said

to Mr. Quinn, "and if she agrees to return with me, you will come back to preside over my library too."

"Oh, yes, your lordship." Mr. Quinn nodded. "And it is to be hoped that she will. She'd not like me telling you this, my lord, but I am quite sure that she is suffering over this situation. Indeed, I am of the opinion that her anguish quite equals your own."

"She has told you so?" Eric questioned eagerly.

"Oh, no, my lord, on the contrary. She has repeatedly told me that she has no feelings for you, none at all, and that she devoutly hopes never to see you again, not in this life! But in my estimation the very repetition of these sentiments give the lie to them."

"I pray you are right, Mr. Quinn," Eric murmured.

"There is the tree," the librarian said in a low voice. "As I explained, it grows very near the water. I think it would be best to approach it from the back."

"If I were to do that, she might see me. I think it is best approached from the front. Though certainly it does grow near the stream, I think I can edge around it and reach her side."

"You had best be careful to watch where you are going, sir, with the weakness in your ankle as well as your leg. There are stones and other hazards about, and it rained the day before yesterday. The earth is still damp and might give way beneath you."

"I will be careful, and it is in a good cause. I do thank you, Mr. Quinn. You had best go back the way you came. In case I am not successful, you could incur her wrath."

"Very well, my lord. You have my hopes for your success."

"I do thank you, and I am quite aware that I hardly merit your help, given my reprehensible accusations on that last day. I need not tell you, I think, how this situation has wrought upon me in all respects."

"I do understand, my lord. You have explained it entirely to my satisfaction," the librarian assured him. He added anxiously, "I pray that you be careful, my lord."

"I will," Eric whispered as he moved away.

He reached the stream, and by dint of walking on the soft sand at the water's edge, he was finally within a foot of the immense oak—a tree he guessed might have been a sapling when Henry VIII was still a prince. The twittering of the myriads of birds would also drown out whatever sound he might make, he decided. It was a pretty place Laura had chosen for herself, an ideal spot to read or to contemplate nature. He looked upward at the sky, seen through the leafy branches of the great tree. They formed a natural lattice far more intricate and beautiful than anything man could devise. Fluttering about him were bright-colored butterflies and dragonflies, with their blue bodies and iridescent wings. In the stream there were swift, darting minnows. Soon he hoped to glimpse Laura's exquisite reflection.

He moved forward quietly, and in a few moments he was standing directly in front of the oak. In another second he would step around that vast trunk to confront her and to beg her forgiveness, and hopefully she would listen.

He winced as he ruefully remembered how he had not listened; remembered, too, her stricken face as he had hurled his furious accusations at her. Yet, he thought defensively, how might he have guessed the truth . . . there was an answer for that! Knowing Laura, knowing the hours she had spent with him, how could he have dreamed that she was merely pretending to comfort him? How could he have imagined that Laura, of all people, could ever be unfaithful?

"Oh, God," he mouthed, and moved forward hastily, too hastily, stepping on a stone that slid away beneath his foot. His bad ankle suddenly twisted, and with a moan of agony he started to fall forward. He made a hasty grab for a nearby bush, but the slender branch broke in his hand and he plunged into the stream, striking his head on something hard. He experienced a blinding pain and then knew nothing more.

Laura had been reading, or rather she had been trying

to read, an episode that was proving far too familiar to enjoy. At the sound of that startled cry and the subsequent splash, she rose hastily to her feet, and stepping to the water's edge, she saw the man lying on his back, borne forward by that strong current.

"Eric!" She gasped in horror, and rushing down to the water's edge, she slipped into the stream, grabbing his coat. His weight pulled her farther into the water, but she was able to clutch hard a sturdy bush by the bank. Then, hooking one foot around the stalk of that bush, she used both hands to pull her unconscious husband up onto the bank. Kneeling beside him, a cry escaped her as she saw a thin, scarlet trickle of blood running down the side of his face. For one horrified moment she feared that he had struck his temple, but a second later, upon carefully running her fingers over his head, she realized that he had sustained no more than a scalp wound. She quickly pulled up a fold of her gown to stanch the bleeding.

"Eric . . . oh, Eric, my dearest," she murmured, and scarcely cognizant of what she was doing, she eased his head onto her lap, smoothing back his wet hair, the while she looked down anxiously into his pale face. "Oh, my dearest, are you badly hurt?" she murmured. "I . . . I must get help," she added fearfully. "Where . . . ?"

"Laura," Eric whispered, opening his eyes and staring at her almost unbelievably. "It . . . is it you?"

"Shh," she cautioned. "You must not be speaking. You are hurt. Your head—"

"I must speak," he said urgently. "I . . . I must tell you how sorry I am. I was sore c-confused and I . . . I came here to find you, here at this oak . . . because you'd not see me, and I have been in torment these last months. My only excuse is that I did not know, but I should have known. She—*you*—were so d-different that night that I played you f-false, but afterward I was glad because she was gone and you were here . . . . It is you, the real you, I came to love, my dearest Laura. Oh, God, God, how can I make you understand?"

"I . . . I think I am beginning to understand, but, my

dearest, you must not talk . . . you have sustained a hard blow. Your head—"

"Damn my head." He looked up at her lovingly. "Laura, please come back to me. I do love you with all my heart. Oh, Laura." He spoke brokenly now. "You have my heart and . . . and a man cannot live without his heart, you know."

Magically her own anger seemed to have disappeared, her anger, her resentment, and what she had believed to be her hatred. Looking into his pleading eyes, it was impossible to doubt him, and equally impossible to ignore the promptings of her own heart.

Consequently there was no suppressing the words that now rose to her lips. "I . . . I expect I will come back to you, Eric, my dearest. I . . ." But whatever else she might have said was silenced, for Eric had clasped his arms around her and pulled her against him, and even though they were now both extremely wet, they subsequently agreed that the kisses that he pressed upon her lips and which she rapturously returned, were quite the most satisfactory that either had ever experienced.

L'ENVOI

THE DAYLIGHT HAD FADED, leaving the sky a pearly gray, but a streak of gleaming brightness still lingered across the western horizon, dyeing the clouds a deep scarlet.

Thus, since it was not yet time to ignite the flames of the midsummer fires, the guests of the Earl and Countess of Marne were still strolling through the magnificent gardens, admiring the beds of summer roses. A group of them had stopped to praise the exquisite outlines of a marble Aphrodite standing in the midst of a planting of pale pink azaleas. Several ladies were frankly envious when told that the ancient and authentic statue had been purchased by their host and hostess in the course of a recent visit to Greece.

Some members of the countess's family also expressed a certain surprise at Laura's constant traveling. Lady Margaret, down from Scotland with her laird, was, of course, only teasing, as was Lady Roswell, but Lady Julia, who had come from Cornwall alone, had been heard to say sharply that she did not understand how a mother of two rambunctious children, neither out of the nursery, could see her way clear to leaving them quite so often.

She had added that it was seldom, indeed, that she left her children to the care of their nurses. Amazingly Julia, barren for the first several years of her marriage, had given birth to two sets of twins in four years!

However, much of the conversation circulating through the garden on that summer evening centered about the coronation, which would be held the following year, George III having died on a frosty day in January, six months previously. The Earl and the Countess of Marne would attend, and so would Margaret and her laird, but Julia had no such plans. She had been heard to remark a trifle crossly that her lord was yet in Toronto, and by this same time next year he again might have returned to Canada.

Consequently, as talk of the coronation ebbed and flowed about her, she was listening with only half an ear to the description of robes that must needs be brought out of storage and hopefully refurbished. There was also some discussion concerning the great numbers of royal personages and foreign dignitaries who would be present. Julia did enjoy hearing about the gowns some of the ladies were planning to have made. The new fuller shapes were very flattering to some figures, but actually, she was mainly thinking about her brother-in-law's enthusiastic greeting.

Eric had been highly complimentary regarding her appearance, telling her that blue was quite her best color. He had also decried the fact that he had seen nothing of her for so many years. Actually he had said "we" but she knew that he was referring to himself alone and subtly letting her know that he had not forgotten a certain enchanted spate of days when they had roamed the countryside without the cloying company of his new-made bride. Indeed, judging from the warmly interested look in his eyes, she could hardly believe that half a decade had passed since last they had met. Was it possible, she wondered excitedly, that he might want to take her on another excursion of the kind they had so enjoyed all those years ago? She glanced about for Laura but did not see her.

Laura, however, was only a short distance away from

Julia's chair. She was coming across the grass with Lady Orville and describing for the latter's benefit their latest visit to London.

"It is such a crowded city, my dear, but the Prince Reg—I must remember to call him King—sent a note to Eric, and of course—"

"And of course you cannot refuse a royal command. I am sure you had a fine time, and certainly you are far too young to become a country mouse, my dearest Laura."

Laura laughed. "My dear Millicent, I am a country mouse who might not want to travel in a London that seems to be more crowded and more noisy by the moment, but I do want to go to Paris in September, which I am told is one of the very best times to visit the city. I have already sent word to Madame Solange that I am coming, and I have described the gowns I wish her to make for me."

"And what does your lord and master say to that?"

"Oh, he is quite willing. Mrs. Dinsdale is so very good with the children, and since I was in my sixth month when we returned from Greece, he says that he does not mind that I will be in my fourth month come September."

"If I were he, I would not mind, either. You did bear your son and daughter with consummate ease. By the way, love, do twins run in your family?"

"No, not in my family," Laura said wonderingly. Then she nodded. "Oh, I see, you are talking about Julia. Her husband's older sisters were twins. Furthermore, her sister-in-law has twin girls."

"I see. From my observation, twins do seem to run in families. Your sister must have had a hard time. She is much changed. I would not have known her."

"Yes." Laura shook her head. "I am sure that having two sets of twins in four years could not have been easy. She is a surprisingly good mother, though, but of course the children do tie her down. She was delighted to come up from Cornwall for the lighting of the midsummer fires."

Lady Orville smiled. "When you told me that you were inviting your sister Julia to see the bonfires, I was amazed at your magnanimity of spirit. However, I had not seen her in some years. Had you?"

Laura, meeting her probing gaze, only laughed. "I will plead not guilty to your not entirely veiled accusations, my dear Millicent. And furthermore, you know very well that we have not seen each other in five years and a little over. Eric is doing his best to make her feel at home. It is very difficult for poor Julia these days—with her husband away so often. There are times when she is very lonely, or so Mama tells me. She says that not a week passes that she does not have a ten-page letter from Julia. And she has never been able to persuade Frederick to leave Land's End and settle down in one of his other estates—say outside of Bath or Worthing."

"Yes, I remember you telling me that they had quite a quarrel over that," Lady Orville commented. She said dryly, "Does she have any inkling of why her husband is away so often?"

Laura rolled her eyes. "I do not believe that Frederick has told her that he has a beautiful young Canadian mistress. Eric found it out purely by accident. And as I have explained to you, he does spend five or six months out of the year with Julia and the children, but he is rarely here in the summer because Canadian winters are very cold. Ah . . ." She moved to Eric, who had just signaled her. "Is it time to light the fires, my dear?" she asked.

"Yes, it is, very nearly." He turned to Julia. "Will you excuse us?"

"Of course, Eric, my dear." The fading and plump little woman at his side gave him a ravishing smile. She turned to Laura. "One of these days, my dearest Laura, I am going to steal your husband and spirit him off to Land's End."

"You will have to give me advance notice so that I can be prepared, my dear." Laura took Eric's proffered arm and winced slightly as he wickedly squeezed her fingers

in the crook of it. She did manage to conceal the smile
that the gesture invited.

Julia, blissfully unaware of this signal, said archly,
"And who will light the bonfires this year?"

"One of the servants. Tommy wanted to do it. He
remains enchanted with the custom, but Eric would not
allow it."

"Who is Tommy?" Julia asked.

"Mr. Thomas Quinn," Laura amplified. "He used to
be our librarian."

"Oh, I think I do remember him. He is not still
working on your library, is he?"

"Oh, no, he is much more importantly employed at the
library in the British Museum. He and Kitty, his wife,
will be staying with us for a fortnight."

"Oh, I see," Julia said, dismissing the subject of Mr.
Quinn. With a slight pout she said, "I had been looking
forward to watching you, Eric. I thought the setting of the
fires was supposed to ensure your luck for the whole of
the coming year. Are you not afraid of challenging the
fates, as it were, my dear?"

"No, not really, Julia." Eric turned to Laura. "Let us
alert the rest of our guests, my darling. You take the
ladies and I will take the gentlemen."

"On the contrary." She giggled and gave him a deliber-
ately provocative look. "You take the ladies and *I* will
take the gentlemen."

He chuckled. "Just which of us are you hoping to
benefit, my love?"

She winked at him. "Shall I allow you three guesses?"

His chuckle turned into merry laughter as he bent to
kiss her on the cheek before strolling away.

Julia looked after him. "Eric is considerably more
attractive than he was five years ago," she observed
thoughtfully.

"Is he?" Laura asked.

"Can you not tell? I would not have sent him out
among the ladies," Julia said pointedly. "I would imagine that many of them are attracted to him."

"I would imagine the same thing, Julia." Laura nodded. "But I trust him and he trusts me."

"If I were you . . ." Julia began.

"But you are not, my dear Julia," Laura said gently, "and I am not you. Now, if you will excuse me, I must go and inform the gentlemen about the lighting of the fires."